Damned
Strong
Love

DAMNED STRONG LOVE

The True Story of
Willi G. and Stefan K.

A NOVEL BY
LUTZ VAN DIJK

*Translated from the German
by Elizabeth D. Crawford*

Henry Holt and Company
New York

For Andrés

This book was made possible by a grant from the August-von-Platen Institute of the Departments of Language and Literature Science of the University of Siegen in Nordrhein-Westphalia. The story is based on the life history of Stefan K., born in 1925, who lives in Warsaw and graciously made himself available to the author for reference at all times.

Henry Holt and Company, Inc.
Publishers since 1866
115 West 18th Street
New York, New York 10011

Henry Holt is a registered
trademark of Henry Holt and Company, Inc.

Translation copyright © 1995 by Elizabeth D. Crawford
All rights reserved.
First published in the United States in 1995 by
Henry Holt and Company, Inc.
Published in Canada by Fitzhenry & Whiteside Ltd.,
195 Allstate Parkway, Markham, Ontario L3R 4T8.
Originally published in Germany in 1991 by
Rowohlt Taschenbuch Verlag under the title
Verdammt Starke Liebe.

Library of Congress Cataloging-in-Publication Data
Dijk, Lutz van.
[Verdammt starke Liebe. English]
Damned strong love: the true story of Willi G. and Stephan K. /
by Lutz van Dijk; translated from the German by Elizabeth D. Crawford.
p.   cm.
Includes bibliographical references (p.   ).
1. World War, 1939–1945—Fiction. 2. Gay men—Europe—
History—20th century—Fiction. I. Title.
PT2664.I48V4713 1995   94-42075

ISBN 0-8050-3770-5
First American Edition—1995
Designed by Debbie Glasserman

Printed in the United States of America on acid-free paper. ∞

10 9 8 7 6 5 4 3 2 1

CONTENTS

Stefan K., age sixteen, in July 1941.
Courtesy Lutz van Dijk.

Damned
Strong
Love

THE LAST SUMMER

JULY 8, 1941. The second summer of war in Poland. A beautiful, really hot day—I'd gone with a few friends to swim in the Vistula after my early-morning job with Max Licht, the German baker.

We arrived at the bank of the river at about noon, our clothes sticking to us in the terrific heat. We hurriedly checked out the area for Germans, including any soldiers who might also be taking advantage of the hot day to swim.

Andrzej, a neighbor boy, was the first to reach the embankment. He threw his small knapsack and his shirt and short pants onto the grass, and disappeared into water over his head. Shortly afterward we joined him in the refreshing stream.

We splashed around in the water, ducking each other and yelling, unaware that two German soldiers were somewhere in the neighborhood. Maybe we were screaming so loudly because we had had so little time to play during the past two years of war and occupation by the German Army.

Each of us had had his own bad experiences. But now, playing in the Vistula, refreshed by the cool, clear water, we forgot all that for the moment.

And it was Andrzej who discovered a branch hanging out over the water and used it, naked as he was, as a springboard. Just as we were swimming toward the bank to get to the branch, a commanding voice suddenly bellowed: "Get out of there, get moving! Every man out of the water at once, and stand still!"

"Every man"—that was brave, skinny Andrzej; little Pavel; his even smaller brother, Marek; and I, Stefan, the tallest of our group. Dripping and shivering with fear, not with cold, we stumbled out of the water and looked toward the gruff voice. Only now did the roundish soldier emerge from behind some thick bushes, along with his companion, who looked even younger. The two Germans pointed their rifles at us.

"You know what happens to partisans in wartime?" the older one yelled before we were even out of the water. We tried to assume some kind of military-looking posture—hard to do when you're dripping wet and stark naked! Since I spoke the best German of the four of us, I timidly asked permission to speak.

"Partisans—the Polish Resistance—sir? We're only children who came here to swim. So please, give us our things and we'll go right home."

The soldier showed a smile, even if it was only a sneering one.

"Oh, 'swimming'—is that what you crooks call your plottings these days? Now, just tell me you don't know it's forbidden to use your Polack language in public."

So that's what he was driving at. I had to refrain from clapping my hands to my head at this nonsense. Yes, it was true, there was a regulation that we weren't allowed to speak Polish in the presence of Germans—but until a few moments ago there hadn't been any Germans around! Maybe the older soldier just thought it was fun to terrorize a few Polish boys. But what was going to happen now?

Luckily, his companion seemed to be losing interest in us. He whispered something in the older soldier's ear, whereupon that one nodded. Then he screamed at us again in his parade-ground voice:

"We'll let you go this time. But note this for the future: There's no Poland anymore! This is now West Prussia and it belongs to the Greater German Reich! Understand?"

Andrzej and I nodded. When we saw that Pavel and Marek were just staring dumbly straight ahead, we poked them in the sides, and they nodded too.

The two soldiers had had enough of us, but they had one last bright idea. They'd caught sight of Andrzej's knapsack, and now they stuffed into it all the pieces of clothing they saw lying around. One of them grabbed a heavy stone and tied that in too. Finally they slung the bulging knapsack as far as they could into the middle of the Vistula, where after letting out a great bubbling blast of air it sank.

Why am I telling this in such detail, anyhow? Afterward it all went rather well again. Marek and Pavel cried a little of course, but Andrzej and I were able, after more than an hour, to pull our knapsack treasure out of the water with a piece of rope. Best of all was that the soldiers had missed Pavel's little box camera, which he'd carefully laid in a shady place before going swimming. And so in the late afternoon, some hundred yards farther along, we took pictures of ourselves. Little Marek was stationed on a hill to watch while the rest of us spread out a few dampened crusts of bread and ate fresh raspberries.

While we sat in the grass in our almost-dry clothes and enjoyed the tasty meal, I couldn't stop thinking about what the soldier had bellowed: *"There's no Poland anymore!"*

There's no Poland anymore! There's no Poland anymore! That sentence is firmly tied in my memory to the day two years previous, in the late summer of 1939, when I learned that I would never again be allowed to go to school. . . .

EARLY SUMMER, 1939. At age fourteen, I'd just graduated from the seventh grade. I'd been quite a good student—I can say that today, as an old man. At least in school there was always something going on. Besides, I really liked to read, and most of all I liked music. In the music room of our school stood an ancient concert grand piano that our cheerful young teacher had inherited from a distant relative and bestowed on us. He could play it so beautifully and with such great feeling that sometimes the whole class missed hearing the bell and forgot to go home.

It was this young Herr Scibarski who one day summoned my father to school and said to him: "Do you know that your son has musical talent? He really ought to go to the upper school so all his abilities can be properly developed!"

"Aha," my father boomed. He scratched the back of his head somewhat uncertainly, then carefully folded and unfolded his battered railroad cap. He looked at me: "And what do you want, boy?"

I was as uncertain as Father, but unfortunately I had no cap to fold. Neither Father nor Mother had learned to read and write properly in the four elementary-school years of their childhood. At least they'd gone to a German school, and so we were raised to be bilingual from early on. Father had later learned the railroad trade at the freight yards in Toruń. Mother had remained an unskilled worker.

Both had taught us the Catholic religion, which from the earliest, I associated with nice and not-so-nice experiences: Every evening before bedtime, Mother prayed with each of us five children. Afterward she always had a few minutes to listen to our large and small cares and counsel us on what should be done about them on the coming day. That was the nice experience.

Not so nice was that every Sunday we were stuck into so-called good clothes for going to church. Not only did the stiff pants and collars scratch our skins horribly, but the moment we were imprisoned in the torture garments, all of Mother's amiability vanished. She would bustle nervously around us, pulling on crooked cuffs and collars and issuing the wildest threats about the tiniest bits of dirt. I could never believe the good Lord wanted that when He created Sunday.

So now I looked at my father helplessly and finally said

something that would most likely have horrified any other poor father who had to turn every penny around twice: "I would love to learn to sing properly and become a singer someday!"

Unlike Mother, who got into panics every now and then because of our lack of money, Father had always preserved a feeling for "the true life," as he called it. "The true life isn't just fields and working and scratching money together," he would sometimes say, to Mother's annoyance, "but the true life, that's the beautiful things." Then he would grin like a schoolboy, and it was left to our imaginations which "beautiful things" he meant at the time. Now I found out that for him, to my good fortune, singing was one of them.

Turning to Herr Scibarski, he said cheerily, "Good, Herr Scibarski, then Stefan should develop his musical talent, shouldn't he?" And he added seriously, "But you must help him a little too! My wife and I will clothe him and feed him, but we can't help him with school."

So it came about that in the summer of 1939 I often sat with Herr Scibarski in his small, dark, rented room while the other children were enjoying their vacation outdoors. I was cramming for the entrance examinations of the Toruń upper school, and Herr Scibarski wouldn't take a zloty from my parents for it, although after all it was his vacation, too.

The entrance examination took place at the beginning of August. I hadn't shut an eye the whole night before, and that morning, pale and with sweaty palms, I slipped through the impressive gateway of the upper school for the first time. Inside there was a note chalked on an easel blackboard:

ENTRANCE EXAMINATION IN DRAWING ROOM. I had no idea where the drawing room was, but I looked around curiously and saw a small group of pale boys going up one of the great staircases. Since there was no one else in the building, I just ran after them.

In the drawing room each person was seated at a table that was a good distance from the next table, so no one could whisper anything. I scarcely remember the faces of any of the other children now. It seemed to me that we all looked the same—at any rate anxiety about the examination had made us all into similarly mouse-gray, intimidated ghosts.

I also have no memory of what was actually on the test, though to this day I can still feel how sweaty my fingers were. I had trouble holding the pencil properly, and all my papers, when I finally handed them in, showed slight ripples from the dampness of my hands. By the end I hardly knew my name.

Of the following two weeks I know only that I went around in complete exhaustion. I kept doing my normal work, like carrying out newspapers and helping a gardener from whom I earned a little for our family, but I did it all numbly. Only thus can I explain how, in that hot summer of 1939, I didn't really take in what was happening all around me.

I awakened from this condition when, during the next-to-last week of August, I finally received the results of the examination. At first it was merely a relief that the time of waiting was over—gradually it also penetrated that I'd passed the exam and was admitted for the new school year.

Father and Mother and even my brother and sisters looked at me so proudly that I was almost a little ashamed. "Just be glad, Stefan!" my father said to me. "One is certainly not a better person because of a better school. But perhaps one has it a little easier in life all the same. . . ."

And Mother, who was usually anxious because of the lack of money, said in a firm voice, "Tomorrow we'll go to the tailor and order you a new school uniform. No one is going to see that you come from a poor family!"

Slowly I thawed out of my numbness. Most of all I rejoiced that my older brother, Mikolai, who really was a much more ambitious person than I was and unfortunately had not been recommended for higher schooling, was not at all hurt or jealous. One evening before we went to sleep, he came over to my bed, knelt down beside it, and laid a small envelope on my pillow.

"Here, take it—I'm already earning a bit of money, and you're going to stay a poor student for a while and can certainly use it!"

In the envelope were a few coins—no large sum, but still enough that I knew he'd had to work for it for almost a week.

"Thanks, Mikolai. I'll never forget this!"

He just thumped me gently on the shoulder. "I'm glad for you, really! You know I'd have loved to go on to school too, but in the last few weeks, sometimes I think these days it's better if a person's learns a trade."

Then he got up and went back to his own bed. In the dark I heard him lie down on the bed without pulling up the covers.

"Mikolai, what do you mean by 'these days'?" I softly called over to him.

"There's so much hate and tension in the world—lately, mainly between Germany and Poland. With big Germany to the west and the big Soviet Union to the east, we're a tiny country caught in the middle. I just hope the politicians will calm down and not carry out their threats."

My older brother rarely said so much at one time. I sensed that he'd come to his own conclusions about life, and suddenly I felt quite naive in my narrow-minded preparations for the upper school—it had become my entire world in the last weeks. I didn't suspect that in just a few days that world would no longer exist.

On August 30, 1939, two days before the beginning of the new school year, my school uniform arrived. The tailor was allowing my parents to pay off the suit in twenty-four monthly installments. Mother insisted that I try it on immediately. Happy and more relaxed than I'd ever seen her around "good clothes," she kept circling me and stroking the "wonderful fabric" on all sides.

"We absolutely must have a picture taken of Stefan on his first school day!" she said, turning to Father, who immediately and enthusiastically agreed.

"Yes, dear, but I've also wanted a picture of you for a long time, and our other children shouldn't be left out."

A brief, grave shadow slipped across Mother's face. Then it passed, and she laughed and said, "Only this one time, though!"

My first school day at the upper school never took place.

Instead it passed into history. On September 1, 1939, we were still lying in our beds, unknowing, when north of our city of Toruń, at the mouth of the Vistula—specifically, in the harbor of Danzig—the German ship *Schleswig-Holstein* fired on the Polish mainland without a declaration of war.

A few hours later the head of the German government, Adolf Hitler, the so-called Führer, announced on the radio: "Since five forty-five this morning we have been returning fire!" In so saying, he lied twice, but the first was probably out of plain ignorance. It was not at 5:45 A.M. but at 4:45 A.M. that the attack in Danzig harbor took place, for which he had given the secret order on the previous day at 12:40 P.M.

The second lie was deliberate: The Germans were mounting an attack, not a defense, as he implied with the words "returning fire." The Nazis themselves had supplied the pretext for the attack: During the night of August 31 there had been an armed attack on German border guards in Gleiwitz. After the war it came out that the attack had been staged by bandits hired by the Germans.

On this morning we were awakened not with the usual gentle shaking by our mother but by the droning of German heavy military aircraft thundering over our houses. Mikolai was first on his feet and stared out the wide-open window at the sky.

"Now it's started, Stefan!" he said softly to me as I stood beside him and saw how he tried to conceal his excitement with deep breathing in and out. His powerful rib cage rose and fell, but he never said another word all morning long.

But Mother was even more agitated. "What's going to

happen now? Dear God, have people finally gone completely crazy?" At some point she remembered what we had planned for the day. "Well, that can't be helped—we have to go to the photographer today! Stefan, you go put on your new school uniform now!"

I looked inquiringly at Father. Silent and grave, he indicated that I should leave him alone with Mother for a little while. Shortly afterward we five children, who were all crouching in the next room, heard Mother sobbing aloud and Father's voice interposing, over and over, sharp and decisive. When they finally came out, Father said, "I'm going over to our neighbors' now. They have a radio, and I hope we'll soon know more details. Comfort your mother— excitement is out of place now."

Mother sat quietly on their bed and sniffled into a handkerchief.

Finally Father came back.

"War! It's actually war! The government has ordered all men to report immediately. There are 120,000 men being called up to defend Warsaw alone. I'm going to report to city hall today." Then he looked at Mikolai.

"I'll stay with Mother," Mikolai said very softly and seriously. He said it with such conviction that Father hesitated only a moment, then gave him his hand with unaccustomed solemnity: "Good, my boy. I can go in peace if I know that you're here!"

My new school uniform remained hanging in the closet that day. It also remained there for the following six weeks. In these weeks some 70,000 Poles died in the fighting. We had no news from Father the whole time. On September 17 the former Polish government fled abroad. They took with them the 116 air-force planes still remaining. Nevertheless many Polish soldiers kept on fighting till the beginning of October, because it was clear to everyone what would happen after the defeat. The last Polish units surrendered on October 6, 1939.

On the evening of October 6, Mother handed me my school uniform from the wardrobe, after carefully wrapping it in a swathe of brown paper.

"Stefan, Polish children are forbidden to attend all the higher schools, and their places are being given to German students. Run to the tailor and tell him the uniform is completely unworn. Since the Germans won't let you or any other Polish children go to school, we can't use this. Maybe he'll take it back and we'll just lose the first month's payment. . . ."

On the way to the tailor's I passed a bar that was patronized mainly by Germans. The happy singing and celebrating inside poured out into the street. It was a mild fall evening, the air like silk, and the birds were just beginning the first notes of their evening songs.

I was going slowly along the street with my package under my arm, my steps heavy, when I heard a man bawling loudly in German: "There's no Poland anymore! Once and for all, folks, there's no Poland anymore!" Then his voice was swallowed up in the jubilation.

It was a mild fall evening, but I no longer enjoyed the beautiful air or listened to the birds singing. If only Father would come home safe soon . . .

HOMELESS

MORE AND MORE often reports came to Toruń of fathers and brothers who'd been killed in the fighting against the German Army, but Father's name was never among them. Had he been wounded? Had he been taken prisoner?

Mother had never before been separated from her husband for long, and she waited through those first days as if paralyzed by terror. She watched the war going on around her like a film. Finally, after a good two weeks, she suddenly got up, energetically brushed her still beautiful long hair, carefully put it up, and said to us children, "Father wouldn't want us to give up!" She paused for a moment and smiled for the first time since he'd left home. "We mustn't stop believing that times will get better for us!"

At first, though, they did not. It was Mikolai who brought the bad news.

"Pavel's brother says that Father has been deported to Germany for forced labor. They were in the same convoy at first, but then the Germans let Pavel's brother go because he was still so young and didn't look strong enough."

"But where, in God's name?" Mother wanted to know. "What city in Germany did they take him to?"

Mikolai shrugged. "I don't know. Germany is big. To some factory for war work, or to a farm. Pavel said this is supposed to be only for the duration of the war. Afterward all the forced laborers will come home again."

We couldn't know then that an end to the war lay far in the future and that scarcely half of all the forced laborers would ever come back to Poland.

Mikolai also reported that the Germans were going to conscript all unemployed young people for forced labor. Turning to me, he said seriously, "Stefan, I have my apprenticeship—but what about you? In the eyes of the Germans you're no longer a student. You've got to start looking for a job right away, tomorrow. It doesn't matter what, only that you have some kind of work!"

But the next morning there was a new scare. Before it was time to get up—it couldn't have been six o'clock yet—suddenly there was a thunderous knocking on our apartment door. Mother stood in the hallway listening, her face pale. Through the closed door we could hear the steps of several soldiers' boots and the doors being struck with rifle butts. Now we understood what they were yelling, too.

"Let's go—open up! You have until noon today to vacate your apartments! From now on decent German families are going to live here. If you don't go voluntarily, we'll remove you!"

Mikolai was about to throw open the door when Mother stopped him. "Wait a minute, son—maybe they'll go away!" Secretly I admired Mikolai's courage: I saw how his eyebrows were drawn together angrily and how all the muscles of his powerful shoulders tensed. No doubt about it—Mikolai, who usually avoided quarrels and fighting, was ready to defend our home. With his life.

Luckily Mother was right. The soldiers bellowed some more commands, but since they only had to demand eviction, and since they obviously still had many houses ahead of them, they moved on without so much as one of our neighbors opening their door.

In the meantime our little sisters had also awakened and come into the hallway drunk with sleep. Little Dana looked at Mother's and Mikolai's sad faces and right away began to cry. Mother took her in her arms and reassured her with gentle words. She asked Mikolai and me to get breakfast. "Then I can pack a few of the most important things for the little children."

Mikolai stopped abruptly on his way to the kitchen and stared bitterly at Mother. "We aren't going to do it, Mama!" But Mother clearly did not intend to argue with him about it. "You do what I said, Mikolai! You're simply thinking like a child now. Do you mean for you and Stefan and me to fight against the soldiers?" With that, she left us standing in the hall and disappeared into the girls' room.

Mikolai didn't say another word the rest of the morning. When it was time for him to leave for work, Mother placed a conciliatory hand on his shoulder. "Father wouldn't have done anything reckless either, believe me. You go to work now and ask your boss if you can help us move at noon. I'll ask Aunt Olga if we can stay with her at first."

Right after breakfast I went to see Aunt Olga, whom I

never liked particularly because she always bragged so much. She lived in another section of the city, alone in a big house since her husband had died two years before. I found her in a state of high excitement.

"This is simply beyond belief! Can you imagine? The Germans intend to put an honest old woman out on the street! Good thing you came by. You can help me with my packing now, Stefan. I can surely stay with you for a few days?"

I had trouble getting away from her again. But under no circumstances did I want to leave Mother and my sisters alone any longer than was necessary. By the time I got home, Mother had all the suitcases packed with clothing and had just begun wrapping dishes in paper and putting them in cardboard cartons. She'd already heard some more news. "A neighbor just told me that we aren't going to be put out on the street—we'll be moved into smaller houses."

A few weeks before, Mother would have received such news with a moderately severe heart attack. Now she mustered all her strength so that she could reassure us. "Look at it this way, Stefan—you really didn't want to go stay with Aunt Olga, and to live a little more crowded for a while isn't the end of the world!"

We would soon find out what "a little more crowded" meant: We had been living in the railroad workers' apartments with Father, Mother, and five children in a simple but roomy three-room apartment with kitchen and bath. Now we had to manage with a single room in an old, rundown farmworkers' building—without running water, not to mention a bathroom. The toilet was in the courtyard, and water also had to be fetched from there and, after being used, taken back and emptied out. We had to leave half the packed cartons in our lovely former home because there was simply no more space in the one narrow room of our new lodgings. The next day German families moved into the railroad workers' building.

Mother did everything she could to dispel our heartache that first night. She was almost a little too cheerful in her effort to convince us that it could have turned out much worse.

"Well, look, old Tadeusz on the second floor had a heart attack with all the moving . . . and the neighbor across the way, she had everything taken from her because they found some kind of writing they said was forbidden . . . and the little one from over the other side, who's expecting her first baby any day now—"

"Stop it, Mother!" Mikolai suddenly interrupted her loudly. "It's already depressing enough without you having to make it worse!"

Mother's mouth dropped open in astonishment. Then she snapped it shut without contradicting Mikolai. She gave him a long, almost tender look.

That first night in the new lodgings, I scarcely closed my eyes. Mikolai also tossed restlessly under his covers for hours. It was damp and musty in the little room. Mother at least appeared to sleep, but perhaps she was only pretending. All at once, as I stared wide-eyed into the darkness, I was conscious of a feeling of overwhelming sadness in my chest. First the sudden separation from Father and now the loss of our home. I felt the tears suddenly running down my cheeks. No one noticed anything.

THE NEXT MORNING Mikolai was the first one up, because he now had farther to go to his job. He hadn't been gone for half an hour before he was standing in the door again and excitedly calling my name. "Stefan, Stefan! Come on, come quickly—get up! There's a job open for a delivery boy at a German baker here in the neighborhood—he was just putting out the sign as I came by!"

As quickly as I could, I slipped into my clothes, ran a damp comb through my hair once, and ran down the street at his side.

I was the first applicant, thanks to Mikolai's fast reaction. The name of the thin, somewhat older, slightly grumpy baker was Max Licht. He looked at me skeptically and asked me about Father and Mother. I told him that Father was still not back from the war and Mother had to feed five children by herself.

"Well, well," he said, and still didn't seem quite convinced. At this moment his wife came into the store—and now the atmosphere really brightened: She was at least twenty years younger than he, had shining blond hair, and extracted a smile not only from her husband but also involuntarily from me.

"Good morning, everyone!" she called out in a firm voice. She even gave me her hand and said cheerfully, "So, you're our new delivery boy! Welcome! What's your name? Stefan? I like that name!"

Her husband cleared his throat and tried to hold her back. "Well, now, slow down a little, the boy has just introduced himself and—"

But she interrupted him, deciding the matter in my favor. "Oh, come on, Max—such a nice-looking boy! That will please all the customers. You aren't going to send him away?"

While she was speaking, she shot me a secret wink. That this wink meant more, I was to learn only later. At the time I was very happy. So there were also helpful Germans who obviously had no prejudice against Poles.

From then on I was the first one up every day, except Sundays. By four thirty in the morning, when it was still pitch-dark in the city, I was knocking on the back door at the bakery. First I sorted the different orders and packed them up. By five thirty at the latest, I left the courtyard on my delivery bike to make my first round.

When I got back from the first trip around seven, Herr Licht and I had breakfast; Frau Licht usually appeared too. Gradually her husband also began to like me—probably because I was reliable and there were never complaints from customers. I'd been with him for about a month when he called me into the back room about noon one day, shortly before quitting time. "Say, Stefan—how many children are there at home? So—five children? Well, well, now, then take these two big loaves along with you. Your mother will be pleased about that, won't she?"

And so it went from that day on. I was always allowed to

take home some of the leftover bread. Extra bread was real treasure at that time, because we Poles had begun receiving food allotted by ration cards. The rations were so small that Mother had difficulty filling our stomachs.

Sometimes Frau Licht also invited me for midday dinner. The couple had no children, and I sensed that it gave her pleasure to spoil me a little. Then sometimes she'd thoughtfully run her hand through my hair and look over at her husband seriously. They knew as well as I did that they were all that kept me from being sent to Germany for forced labor. After all, I was now fifteen years old.

Occasionally the mistress also sent me shopping. Since I'd become known in the neighborhood, I was allowed into the German shops; everyone knew I wasn't getting things for our family but for the German couple at the bakery. Now and then Frau Licht also gave me a letter, which I delivered to a young journeyman locksmith for a few months and then every so often to a student. "Max doesn't need to know about this!" she'd say conspiratorially. "This is my private affair."

It must have been sometime in the fall of 1940 that I had an unpleasant experience with some German boys, who now were wearing the uniform of the Hitler Youth: short dark pants with a belt and hunting knife, as well as a brown tunic with a neckerchief. I must confess that to have so many friends and companions, I would gladly have worn something like that.

On this particular day I was coming back from the butcher's with a full shopping basket for Frau Licht and still had to go to the student's to deliver a letter. I was scarcely out of the store when three Hitler Youths, who couldn't have been much older than I was, marched right up to me. There wasn't time to run away. The first of them, a skinny beanpole of a boy with brown curls, started right in: "Say, Polack, what do you mean by shopping there? You are a Polack, aren't you?"

I held the heavy basket firmly in both hands and said nothing. Perhaps they would only spit out their slogans and then let me go. But then the second one, a little guy with glasses, let loose: "Maybe your filthy mother didn't teach you any manners, huh?" And as he spoke, he shoved me so that the topmost package fell out of the basket into the dirty street.

When I went to pick it up, the third one gave me a kick from behind. I didn't fall, but the shopping basket slipped out of my arms and everything fell to the ground. As if by reflex, I grabbed the one nearest to me—I think it was the one with the curls—tore the kerchief from his neck, and slapped him hard in the face.

The three of them went crazy: They hit and kicked me until I felt the blood spurt out of my nose, run down my face and neck, and drip onto my white baker's jacket. I tried to defend myself as well as I could. But one of them could always attack from behind, so it probably would have turned out really badly if the butcher's wife hadn't come out of the shop and stopped the fight. She seemed more concerned about the annoyance to her customers than anything, though, for when the group was gone, she didn't even glance at me but just angrily slammed the door to her shop.

When I'd gathered up the dirtied packages again, I

noticed to my horror that the letter from Frau Licht had landed in a puddle and was soaking wet. The ink of the name on the envelope had run, and I was afraid that it wouldn't look much better inside. Naturally I'd known the address of the student long since, but how would he react to my mishap?

I used my once-white jacket, which was now filthy anyway, to do the necessary cleaning on my face and then laid it on top of the basket. Shortly afterward, I rang the doorbell of the young man, with whom I'd never before exchanged more than a brief greeting. When he opened the door and caught sight of me, at first he looked shocked, then concerned.

"What did they do to you? Come right in and sit down!"

But I stood there anxiously and first showed him the now-filthy letter. "I was attacked by HY boys—that's how the letter fell in the muck. I'm sorry. . . ."

He looked deep into my eyes for a long moment. Then he took hold of my shoulder and pulled me into the room. There he poured some red wine into a glass and handed it to me. "Here, drink this—it will warm you. . . . The bandits! Basically they're all poor youngsters, but now they have a few medals and ribbons, they can give a few orders, and they act as if they're Emperor Nero in ancient Rome!"

I was speechless. I'd never heard such words from the mouth of a German. He really and truly thought the way I'd been treated was unjust!

"You know," he then continued thoughtfully, "you aren't a child anymore, and you've probably known for a long time why your boss's wife sends me letters now and then, haven't you? No, no, it's not a great love, not that. . . . But old Licht isn't a particularly tender man, and since I often feel lonely here. . . . Well, that's life sometimes. . . ."

Of course, I'd already drawn my own conclusions. But I couldn't really feel any indignation about it, although I knew from my religion that it wasn't permitted for them to meet secretly and for me to play messenger. Still, I had liked Frau Licht from that first moment, when she winked at me— and I found myself attracted to the young student, who had a gentle, kind face and a sturdy, masculine body, in a manner that disturbed me.

I was moved by the great trust he showed me and made up my mind not to betray them for anything in the world. Before I left, he gave me a few lines to the baker's wife in which he briefly told her what had happened.

"Don't worry, she won't scold you!" he said reassuringly as we parted. "And if you ever need help, if you're bothered again, now you know where to come!"

How did it happen that this young man thought so differently from most Germans? And how was it possible that he wasn't in the service, like everyone else his age by this time?

I would never find out, because a short time later he suddenly disappeared. My mistress seemed to have forgotten him too. In any case, she didn't exhibit any sad feelings. But I couldn't get him out of my head for a long time.

STIRRING
FEELINGS

I N JANUARY 1941, three experiences occurred one after the other that changed my life forever. I had my first row with Frau Licht; I turned sixteen; and . . . ah, the third. . . .

After the student's sudden disappearance, I had no more letters to deliver for a while. However, one morning, at the beginning of 1941, when her husband had just disappeared into the back room, Frau Licht again winked at me in the familiar way and slipped an envelope into the side pocket of the shopping basket. I didn't give it any further thought and, as usual, went to the appropriate address on my return home.

When I knocked at the house door, a plump young woman opened it. I was so surprised that at first I couldn't get out any suitable words and tried to leave again with a murmured apology. But she'd already caught sight of the envelope with the name on it and commanded excitedly, "So, young man, kindly give me the letter—my husband has no secrets from his wife!"

My face went as red as if *I* had written a love letter to her husband. I looked into the house in search of help, but he was nowhere to be seen.

While I was still trying to keep the letter in my hands and somehow get away, she suddenly grabbed my arm and bit my wrist so hard that I involuntarily opened my fist, and the now badly crumpled letter fell to the ground. Instantly she bent and snatched it.

"You all must think I'm a little stupid, hey?" she screamed in a mixture of triumph and despair, without paying any attention to some passersby who were looking uncertainly in our direction. Yes, but now was it she who was stupid or her husband—or my boss's wife, who obviously hadn't known of the existence of this determined woman before?

The one sure thing was that I would get in trouble. Crestfallen and perplexed, I stood in front of the deceived wife. Any impulse to flee had disappeared. She didn't know what to do with me either, now that she was holding in her hands the proof of her long-held suspicion. For a moment she looked almost pityingly at my arm, on which the bleeding bite marks were now clearly visible.

"I hate men who are too cowardly to tell the truth!" she finally informed me and then slowly, almost thoughtfully, closed the door. I couldn't deny a certain sympathy for her, in spite of her powerful incisors. But now it was necessary to gently prepare Frau Licht for any possible consequences.

After the noon meal, when we finally had a few minutes alone without the baker, I rolled up my shirtsleeve to exhibit my wounds, in order to temper her personal disappointment somewhat. In fact she'd had no idea of the existence of that woman. Now, however, she was desperately anxious that her own, still completely unsuspecting husband would find out something.

"Did she ask your name? Or who you worked for?"

It was certainly lucky that she signed her letter only with a pet name and otherwise used no return address. The deceived wife hadn't looked at the letter at all in my presence. Still somewhat pale, but already with a cool logic that I'd never seen in her before, she said suddenly, "Stefan, my boy—you can't possibly stay here with us! If the woman finds out that you work for us, then . . . no, that just won't do!"

I'd had a feeling that someday a punishment for my message-carrying would fall on me. Just as spontaneously as she'd allied herself with me that first time, now it was logical to her that I must go. I didn't figure my chances were very good, and I couldn't and wouldn't betray her to her husband. I slunk home very sadly that noontime.

A few days passed without Herr Licht calling me in to be fired. Maybe she'd had second thoughts?

Finally, after well over a week, one morning early, as soon as I'd entered the back room, he murmured in my direction, "Come here a minute, Stefan." We were almost always alone at this time. I couldn't read any particular excitement in his face. Finally he began to mumble indistinctly, "Well now, I've no idea why my wife has nothing good to say about you all of a sudden. She simply won't come out and say it clearly. . . ."

He looked searchingly at me. I remained silent and subdued and looked down at the floor. Let him think I'd broken something. I simply could not tell him the truth.

"So, so," the mystified man murmured, but he appeared to have arrived at a decision. I struggled to hear his soft voice over the crackle of the freshly lit ovens next to us. "Well then, you stay here! All the customers are satisfied, and I'm satisfied with you too. What's all the bleating about? You know how very much I love my wife, but sometimes, well, sometimes I have to say that she doesn't understand much about business. . . ."

The last words were almost spoken to himself. What a relief!

I hadn't said anything at home about the impending calamity. But now I went on the alert again and began to look around for some other work. Frau Licht was still not without influence over her husband, and who knew how long he'd remain firm.

MY SIXTEENTH BIRTHDAY was coming up. The previous year we hadn't celebrated any birthdays at all, because we were still so concerned about Father that we couldn't have celebrated properly without him. But at the beginning of 1941, Mother said we would celebrate again, even without big presents. And my birthday was the first on the calendar.

Everyone was still sleeping on the morning of my birthday when I got up and zipped off to work. But twice the day before, Mother had sent me out of the room, saying with a mysterious smile, "Because of tomorrow!" So on that day I couldn't get home from work fast enough.

Mother had baked a tiny birthday cake, with a real white

candle in the middle. "It's more of a candle stand made out of dough than a cake, dear boy, but it's made with real sugar and it's the recipe that you used to like so much."

With a stern look at my little sister, she added, "And Dana has absolutely promised not to beg, so you can have your little cake all to yourself!" Dana looked at us both with her huge, innocent eyes, ready to keep the promise for at least two minutes. We all three had to giggle. Oh, and to think it used to be like that all the time!

Shortly afterward we all sat down to eat together, except for Mikolai, who didn't get home from work until later. Mother had laid an almost new white shirt at my place, which she'd tied with a red ribbon—red and white, the now prohibited Polish national colors. Mother and I looked at each other, but we didn't say anything in front of the younger children.

"The shirt is Father's, but he wore it only once—do you like it?" she asked me softly.

"Yes, very much, Mamushia!" I answered, also softly, "and the ribbon too."

In early evening, when it was already dark outside, Mikolai came home. He gave me a long, hearty hug and then pressed a small card into my hand. In colored letters he'd printed on the front: INVITATION. And on the back he'd written:

Dear big little brother! When I was sixteen, Papa took me to a pub for the first time. And though we're not supposed to be on the street at night anymore, I'd like to take you out tonight. It's a surprise! Yours, Mikolai.

I sensed that Mother didn't like Mikolai's idea. But she wouldn't forbid us to do it. So she just gazed after us anxiously when we left the house after seven o'clock.

Frozen snow crunched under our shoes. Mikolai was in a hurry. Soon we left the main road and turned into a little path. After less than a hundred yards it became so dark that I could hardly see Mikolai. I only heard his steps and his quiet, deep breathing. Utterly trustful, I ran along behind my big brother. At one point he said, "It's a good night. The moon hardly shows through the cloud cover, and no one can see us."

Suddenly he stopped and carefully placed his hand over my mouth. There wasn't a sound audible—even the wind had died down, and the dark silhouettes of the trees stood motionless in the night.

"It's all right!" he whispered. "Come on!"

As he spoke, he took me by the hand and pulled me into a thicket on whose other side heavy fir boughs covered a wide wooden board. Mikolai moved the board to one side almost soundlessly and shoved me forward into the opening. It went down quite steeply into a small underground room, though I didn't take in its size until after Mikolai had carefully shoved the board back into place and lit a candle: The space must have been some six feet by six, and along one wall heavy wooden crates were piled to the ceiling. The room was just high enough so that we could both stand upright in it. I was astonished that it was relatively warm, although outside the temperature was certainly below freezing.

"Well, how do you like our little nightspot?" Mikolai asked with his voice only slightly lowered. From his right pocket he took a small bottle of schnapps, from the left two glasses. "Well, little brother, what do you say now?"

On the one hand I was touched at how lovingly he'd arranged everything—on the other I couldn't completely suppress a feeling of alarm: Mikolai obviously had contacts with the partisans—that meant he was consciously risking his life. And he'd never spoken with Mother or me about it!

"Mikolai—how long have you been with them?" I needed to know before I could clink glasses with him.

"Honestly, Stefan, I'm not with them. I helped Pavel bring a crate here one time recently. And that was only because someone else didn't show up and Pavel didn't have time to find anyone else he could trust."

"But what if someone finds us here now?"

"We're completely secure tonight! Pavel told me that the hiding place is changed every few days. This one here will be used just this week and then closed down. . . ." I felt that Mikolai knew more than that but didn't want to make me uneasy.

In the meantime he'd filled our glasses and handed one across to me. A peculiar excitement had seized us both—I saw that his hand trembled slightly as we touched glasses without a word. Once when I was little, Father had given me a swallow of schnapps when I was sick. Now Mikolai was repeating a ritual with me that he had experienced with Father. I found the burning feeling in my throat less than pleasant. Actually the taste was rather nasty, but the warmth that soon spread through my belly felt good.

We both took off our thick jackets, sat on them, and

opened our top shirt buttons. Mikolai was now almost eigh-
teen and already had short dark hair on his chest and arms
and legs. He'd been shaving every morning for at least two
years. I still had no beard worth mentioning, only a few
feeble stubbly hairs that I shaved off with his razor every now
and again. When he wasn't there.

Mikolai poured a second time. He still had something on
his mind, I could see that. But I could wait. I looked at his
profile in the flickering candlelight and suddenly thought
that he had something noble about him—like a young Polish count, or no, like one of the young saints who was
pictured as a martyr in a side aisle of our church. . . .

"Do you daydream about girls sometimes too?" The young
saint finally came out with it. I didn't dare say that I'd just
been daydreaming about him.

"You know, Stefan, when I was your age, Father told me
that you shouldn't think of such things until marriage. But I
simply have to talk to someone about it. I can't help thinking
about girls all the time: Girls who undress in front of me, who I
can touch, who I can press against me. I'm going absolutely
crazy with it. I can't possibly talk to Mother about it."

My attentive silence seemed to Mikolai to indicate un-
spoken understanding. Ordinarily so quiet, he talked non-
stop.

He filled our glasses again and then laid a hand on my
shoulder. "Stefan, you're closer to me than anyone else in
the family. I've often helped you. Now I need your advice,
your honest answer: Do you also have feelings like mine?
Would you also like to sleep with a girl?"

What was Mikolai talking about exactly? Yes, damn it, I was sixteen years old as of today, and naturally I'd heard other boys talking about girls from way back. But that had been mere joking or bragging. I would usually think at those times, Oh well, that will all come later, later when you're grown up. Then the grown-ups drive each other crazy and call it love. I simply hadn't felt I was capable of something like that.

But what about that strange feeling for the student that time? Did Mikolai perhaps mean something like that? Sort of a prickly feeling in the belly, enthralling and liberating at the same time, a tremendous attraction to another person, the wish to be able to touch him?

Mikolai was talking himself into more and more of a fury, his dark eyes flashing, and more and more often he touched me, struck me on the knee, pressed my hand to emphasize his words—with brotherly affection. I fell more and more under his spell: He spoke in glowing words of naked girls, of breasts and thighs—I saw his powerful arms, could look at his manly chest in his opened shirt, and wished that he would clasp me firmly in his arms and never let me go. . . .

Suddenly he stripped off his shirt and opened the top buttons of his trousers. His skin was gleaming wet with sweat. Completely spellbound, I stared at the almost mechanically efficient movements of his hand, in which he held his penis.

"Come on, Stefan!" I heard his oddly husky-sounding deep voice. "Come on, we'll do it together—since you think exactly the way I do."

I did nothing. I felt my own penis get stiff—it wasn't the

first time—but only today had I found out the secret of this physical change.

What had formerly been strange and incomprehensible to me became clear all at once—I wasn't especially late or slow to develop. It simply had nothing to do with me—the jokes of the other boys, the silly fuss between grown-up women and men. It was all wrong—wrong for me.

Looked at superficially, it was all wrong in this absurd situation in the hideaway, too, although through Mikolai I got the answers to my questions. Everything that he'd told me so trustingly about girls, I felt exactly the same toward him. I saw how he closed his eyes ardently when he was at the high point of excitement. I also closed my eyes and saw him, my half-naked, brave, reliable, loving, big brother Mikolai—this beautiful man.

Honestly, it wasn't cowardice that kept me from telling him then that I didn't dream of naked girls at all but of him. I was simply so overwhelmed that I didn't want to detract from this moment of enlightenment with ridiculous, stammering explanations. Besides, I had such boundless faith in Mikolai that I simply couldn't imagine that he would reject anything I felt.

MIKOLAI FILLED OUR glasses one last time. We realized it must be long after eight o'clock. Mother would surely be worried by now.

"Now you're a man!" Mikolai said, and by now the schnapps was influencing his speech. My head was spinning too, but at the same time I was wide-awake.

"Yes, I had a good time being out with you, Mikolai!" I said, more to myself than to him.

The trip home was without incident. We saw Mother standing in the window when we turned our corner. Without a harsh word she gave each of us a good-night kiss, as she always did. "Did you have a good time?"

I lay awake for a long time. With the unwonted alcohol, my whole body seemed to float gently. "Now I'm a man." kept going around in my head, "Now I'm a man."

But when it came right down to it, I didn't know what I was supposed to make of Mikolai's statement: I was no man the way he meant it. I was a man who thought about other boys or men. And I knew what everyone I knew thought of such feelings. I shivered.

With fear—but also with joy: Finally I knew what was different about me. And that was a good feeling.

NIGHTS IN
THE CITY

HOWEVER MUCH I looked for a new job in the following weeks and months, I had no luck. At least Frau Licht didn't drop any new insinuations about the need to fire me. But our relationship was no longer the same as it had been, either. She treated me correctly, but with noticeable distance.

Then, in the summer of 1941, things began to change. Around the beginning of June we began to observe increased troop movements of the German Wehrmacht into Poland. Officially these were said to be military maneuvers, and the directions of the various movements weren't consistent enough to figure out. However, anyone with his eyes open could see that the Germans were again sending more soldiers to Poland.

Had there already been successful partisan uprisings in the country? Mikolai said nothing, and anyhow I believed him when he said that he didn't know anything precisely. Nevertheless, a certain unease would not go away.

Then—suddenly—it started. On every main thoroughfare in the country there were units of the German Wehrmacht marching, driving, and riding toward the east. That could only mean one thing: war with the Soviet Union!

From then on, all the regulations and laws against us Poles were enforced to the letter. Anyone even under suspicion was taken into preliminary custody, and three young men who'd been sentenced as partisans were hanged on a gallows in front of the city hall in order to intimidate us. It was during this period that I had the experience with the two German soldiers who surprised me and my Polish friends while we were swimming.

While every day was filled with suffering and fear, for me that summer marked the first of a series of lucky accidents that would lead to the greatest happiness of my life. But of course I couldn't know that at the time.

It all started when, on my morning round as a delivery boy, I passed the Toruń City Theater, as always. By chance my glance fell on the posters and display cases of this gorgeous building, which I always looked at with interest. Still, it wasn't the pictures in the advance notices for the new season that made me stop, but a not particularly large sign beside the right-side entrance: CHORUS SINGERS WANTED.

Immediately I turned my bike around and rode directly in front of the placard. Yes, it was true—Poles could apply too, of course only as extras, in some cases as walk-ons, but still! My old dream of singing—might it become a reality despite these dreadful times?

After work that day I didn't go right home at noon but

hurried straight to the Toruń Theater. Besides me, a crowd of other young women and men had also shown up, and my courage began to fail immediately. How could I hold my own against so much competition? Most of them were older and probably had more training than I did. I'd only sung in our elementary-school choir with Herr Scibarski. Nevertheless—I'd at least try it now, and bravely I wrote my name on the long list of applicants.

A little later a fat man with wavy gray hair came to us in the lobby and asked us to please be patient. "Ladies and gentlemen! You will shortly be divided into small groups and then will have the opportunity to show your talent—"

"How many are you going to take, all told?" He was interrupted by a middle-aged woman with lots of gold chains, who was pulling a shy young woman, probably her daughter, along behind her.

"Madam," the fat man turned toward the impatient mother with slight irritation, "in this house, quality is what counts, not quantity!" The poor thing, I thought, she's certainly lost already.

The actual auditions went relatively fast. I was in a group of six other tenors that was sent to a small room on the second floor of the theater. There a pleasant man in shirtsleeves was waiting for us and, without telling us his name, introduced himself as a staff member of the house. He was in his early thirties at most and appeared to be the chorus director. He took each one of us in individually. I was the first in line.

"Where have you sung before?" he wanted to know first.

"At home!" I answered truthfully, and at the same time

was frightened because it shot through my mind that he might possibly find the answer impertinent.

But he responded, without batting an eyelash and with a friendly grin, "Me too!"

Then he asked me to sing a German song in my register. Since I'd always done well with Herr Scibarski with "At the Well by the Gate," I knew what to sing. And unlike when I took the horrible entrance examination to the upper school, I felt no anxiety in the presence of the nice man and could freely give my best.

"Beautiful," he said seriously when I'd finished, "really beautiful. You have a voice for which something ought to be done. You know that here in the German theater we can use Poles only as extras, but if you can combine your work with us with your other job, I'll gladly take you on!"

It suddenly hit me that during our whole discussion he'd used the polite form for "you." Most Germans hadn't done that for a long time. Happily I thanked him.

"Wait, one more thing!" he called as I was going out the door. "Practice for newcomers is every afternoon at two o'clock, except on Sundays. The performances begin at eight and last until about eleven. As a Pole, you must get a night pass from the management when you get your employment contract from us. Please don't forget that—for your own sake."

Beside myself with joy, I ran home through the city. I didn't see the German soldiers and their motor vehicles, nor the hungry Polish children and the anxious eyes of their mothers.

I thought our old Polish city of Toruń, now called by the

German name of Thorn, was beautiful with all its Gothic churches and castles, and with its monument to the famous astronomer Copernicus in the Old Market. I thought it beautiful in a way that I hadn't since the day we'd had to leave our home.

When I came home so very late that day, Mother was by no means as thrilled as I was. "But, boy, your good job with Herr Licht! How will you manage it—mornings up at four and not in bed until midnight? Oh no, please think this over again calmly!"

"But wait a minute, Mamushia," I argued. "I'm just so happy about the chance for voice training that I'll certainly have more strength for it! Besides, I've been sixteen for a long time!"

She looked at me with concern, but then she smiled and said in mock resignation, "How can I stop you, boy?"

For the first few days I said nothing at the bakery of my new, secondary occupation. However, after two weeks in the theater, I felt so exhausted that I sometimes thought the basket would slide right out of my hand or I'd fall asleep on my bicycle. It didn't escape the baker that a change had taken place in me. But as long as I was punctual and reliable, he left me me alone.

Though getting up so early had become a real burden, I could hardly wait to get to the theater. There, an entirely different world opened to me for the first time in my life!

Most of all it was the people who fascinated me. Many of them were outspokenly unconventional for the time, conducted mysterious relationships, or could tell life stories full of adventure.

There was also a ballet company in the house, whose rehearsals I particularly enjoyed watching. In the meantime it became clear to me how very much I enjoyed looking at boys' and men's bodies.

My first stage appearance was in *The Gypsy Baron* by Johann Strauss. As a member of the chorus, I was permitted to stand on the stage with the old Gypsy Czipra, who in the operetta appoints the young Barinkay to be baron of her band. My admiration for the singer playing the role of Sándor Barinkay, a young tenor at most in his mid-twenties, was boundless.

During my few extra hours at home on Sundays, I'd tell Mother and Mikolai of my experiences in the theater. While Mother enjoyed listening, I noticed that Mikolai shared in the fun less and less. Was he jealous that I had hardly any time for him?

Once he lit into me when I'd just described a particular scene from *The Gypsy Baron* to Mother. "Do you know what the Nazis do to those supposedly jolly Gypsies in Germany and in the countries they occupy? They lock them up, they beat up the men, send them to work camps, and they separate the women and children. Quit your fairy tales—wake up, little brother!"

I was shocked by his vehemence, but I wasn't ready to let the joy I'd finally found in my daily life be destroyed. "D'you think they're all idiots in the theater? They know it isn't reality too. But we at least try to give people a little pleasure and to make the world a little pleasanter."

Mikolai remained unappeased—in fact my words just made him angrier. "You're throwing sand in people's eyes.

Who are you playing for, anyhow? Just for the Germans, who have everything going for them anyway. After all, there are just three Polish extras, and that will last only until the famous German men return from battle."

In my deepest innards I felt that Mikolai was right. If Germany defeated the Soviet Union, then all the "eastern peoples" would be enslaved, and certainly no Polish employees would be tolerated on the stage any longer. But hadn't I found the people in the theater mainly sympathetic and intelligent? Wouldn't they fight Nazi laws?

I told Mikolai about the nice choral director, Herr Werner, who'd hired me and who had since then personally taken real pains with my musical training. "D'you think he'd do that if he believed that garbage about the German master race and the other subhumans? And lots of others in the theater think the way he does!"

Mikolai looked at me grimly. He'd had to swallow too much humiliation in the past two years, and Father still wasn't home. Suddenly I could sense how Mikolai was battling against the growing feeling—we both felt it—that our lifelong close relationship was in grave danger. Without beating around the bush, I demanded earnestly, "Mikolai, do you think I'm a traitor?"

We gazed steadily at each other without saying another word for a long time. At last Mikolai turned away with a resigned wave of his hand:

"You shouldn't rely too much on your new friends in the theater, you know—most of them there are queers anyhow!"

That hurt. I had to turn away not to let him see how wounded I was by the scornful tone of his voice. This wasn't the first time I'd heard the word, but it could only have such effect from the mouth of my brother.

Since that birthday evening in winter I'd wanted again and again to speak with him about it—my longing for boys and men, which I could have confessed first only to him. There simply had never been a suitable opportunity to speak.

Now I felt abandoned by my big brother. Until a few minutes ago, I'd never have thought that was possible. What did he know about queer men anyhow? Did my brother believe that garbage about how all homosexual men can be recognized immediately—as clowns in women's clothes, or as affected aesthetes?

Mikolai had long ago left the room while I still stood in a daze. The first crack in our relationship had appeared. Suddenly I was uncertain whether I should ever tell him anything at all. I sensed with utmost clarity how very much we'd grown apart. For the first time in my life, I thought: I may have to see if I can get along without him.

BUT IT WASN'T that bad yet. First another change took place. One day the rumor went around that the wholesale crude-oil business of the German firm Krieger and Sons was hiring boys fourteen and older who'd be used as so-called worker apprentices to replace men who'd been sent off to Germany.

For a few days I was uncertain what to do. This was the first job with a German firm I'd heard of in months, and I could get an apprenticeship. But there was also the danger I could be sent just about anywhere after the apprenticeship was finished.

Finally I applied for an entirely personal reason: Work at the firm started at seven thirty, and for apprentices the day ended at four o'clock. Krieger wasn't very far from us, so I would be able to sleep until seven every morning. Since rehearsals now began at five in the afternoon, I could do both jobs without constantly having to exceed the limits of my endurance.

Of course, this wasn't any work I'd dreamed of doing. I saw how the workers were completely greasy and dirty by morning break. At least there were showers at the factory, which even the apprentices were allowed to use at the end of the workday.

When I'd signed my new work contract, I informed Herr Licht and his wife that as of next month I would no longer be working for them as delivery boy.

"So, so," he said seriously, without the least unfriend-liness. "Have you thought it over carefully? We've protected you all these months from labor deployment somewhere else. And we'd certainly continue to do that, wouldn't we?"

He'd directed the last question to his wife more than to me. Frau Licht was silent. However, the baker didn't stop. "Yes, we would! But in the meantime you've become a young man. You must know what you're doing. So?"

I stuck with my decision, although I wasn't a hundred percent sure myself. Still, I really did have some things to thank both of them for. I said that to them too when I was leaving. Most of all I had a bad conscience about Mother, when I realized that from now on the extra bread ration would stop.

As if he'd read my thoughts, Herr Licht held on to my hand a moment longer as we parted and said so softly that only I could hear it, "Don't mention it, Stefan—we thank you too! You were the most reliable delivery boy we've ever had. And tell your mother: If she ever doesn't have enough to eat, she should send your little sister over here. Perhaps we won't have any bread then, but there will always be rolls. . . ."

Frau Licht also gave me her hand and even dared a smile in farewell, after she'd been so distant the past months. "Watch out, you handsome fellow!" she teased as I was going through the door.

I suddenly had to smile too. "What for?"

"For the women, for instance!" she called back, almost boisterously. "I know what I'm talking about. . . ."

Indeed. It was nice that we could laugh lightheartedly once more as we parted. Surely a stone would fall from her heart when I was finally gone, and with me the danger of her being discovered.

Still, basically she'd liked me the whole time. At least I could now see that clearly.

THE NEW JOB was no picnic. But I'd known that beforehand—and besides, my real job, the one toward which I directed all my concentration and energy, was at the theater. The rehearsals with Herr Werner, the practice with the others in the chorus, the makeup and costumes, and finally the moments onstage close to great artists. Lighthearted and happy, I often went home at night through the streets of the city humming or whistling cheerfully.

When I was standing all day on the factory floor—the heavy oil smell in my nose, my arms smeared black up to the elbows—more and more often I succeeded in turning my thoughts away from the factory floor to the stage of the theater. I stood at my workbench with my eyes open and my hands mechanically and reliably performing my job—but my spirit was elsewhere, in Vienna at the courts of kings or in front of the towers of an Italian castle.

In the interests of honesty I must add that now and then my thoughts and feelings were very much concentrated in the Toruń factory building as well. Specifically after work, when we boys from the training section showered and I got some very solid information about various techniques for self-stimulation.

While under the shower itself nothing ever happened, though the chatter, when there was any at all, was entirely about girls. But there were various small cubicles for drying and dressing, which sometimes had to be shared by two or three boys. Most of the talk there was about whose penis was biggest—some experts knew the measurements of half the training section.

I often took part and found their comradely games quite funny. But my longings went in a different direction.

While some of the boys would then depart for an evening of cardplaying or to other social life, I rushed right home to change and get to the theater. There, finally, I could sink into the other, incredible, but for me the only true world.

After a few weeks, I had established a good rhythm so that I could handle both activities without becoming particularly exhausted. Although winter had come again, the cold bothered me much less than the year before. This season, in *The Birdseller*, I had only a small role, but it was nevertheless a nice one, which lasted just until intermission. Then I would often help out a little backstage. The theater had become my second home.

If I got home earlier, I found it not particularly comfortable there, since my brother made me aware that he still didn't like it that I had so much to do with Germans. A short time before, one of his friends had even asked him whether I was collaborating with the Germans, because I came home only at night. Mother told me that he'd defended me to the others. But it certainly hadn't pleased him.

Now that I was an apprentice at the factory, I couldn't bring Mother bread anymore, but in several stores in the city there were things that could be bought without ration cards, primarily by Germans, of course. Some of these stores even stayed open until late at night.

After I tried it once and everything went well, I regularly shopped in these stores and brought home to my mother and sisters things that most Poles hadn't been able to get for a long time. The store owners clearly thought I was German, since few Poles were on the street at that hour. My German was now so good that my Polish accent was barely noticeable. Mother was very happy about all the things I brought home. Time and again she would say I should also think of myself and not spend everything on my sisters and her. Mikolai said nothing.

The buying itself gave me pleasure. Sometimes I strolled along by the unlighted display windows long after all my money was spent, just because I loved seeing the few items recognizable in the semidarkness. It was on such an evening in November 1941, specifically on November 4 at ten o'clock, when it happened.

I'd just looked over the display of a large appliance store and was about to wander across the station plaza toward home when somehow I felt myself being watched. The blackout in effect since 1940 wasn't yet observed all over the city. When I looked around, however, I didn't see anyone. Near the main entrance to the railway station I slowed my steps and finally stopped under the lighted globe of a gas lamp, as if I were checking something in my shopping bag.

A moment later he went past me, less than six feet away, then turned briefly and looked me directly in the eye, without a trace of shyness.

At first I saw only his face—his very large brown eyes, his fine-cut nose, and his well-formed lips.

Then, still walking away, he turned around a second time and smiled encouragingly. I saw gleaming, slightly crooked teeth and stared back at him without moving from the spot. Only now, at the second look, did I begin to take in his whole form.

I was badly shaken when I realized that the gorgeous young man, who couldn't have been much older than I, was wearing a uniform and had a visored cap on his head. He was a German soldier!

And there was no doubt about it: He meant me. He had

been following me for quite a while already. Never had anyone looked at me like that. Never had I been so fascinated. At that moment it seemed to me that the only possibility was to remain standing there forever. The end. Lights out. Curtain. What else could happen?

THE
SECRET
SHED

***

MY HEART WAS thumping like crazy. I was involuntarily squashing the old shopping bag in my hands. Only when it suddenly burst in a worn spot and a jar of marmalade fell into the soft snow did my paralysis loosen, and I bent like a robot for the jar, without taking my eyes off the young German.

He'd openly watched my mishap and now remained standing some sixty feet away. He smiled again, this time sympathetically, and gestured with one hand to inquire if he could help somehow. Immediately I shook my head. I was sure he thought I was a German boy and would have me arrested if he found out that I was a Pole.

Finally I had myself under control again. I stuffed the marmalade jar into my jacket pocket with exaggerated self-confidence and clutched the split shopping bag carefully under my arm. I looked fixedly in his direction once more without even the slightest hint of a smile. Then I turned and went off in the opposite direction.

With stiff steps I walked to the edge of city's center. Here the light from the few gas lamps was dim. A peculiar trembling in my hands simply would not go away.

Only now did I realize that I'd walked in the wrong direction. I would have to turn around and go back if I still wanted to get home tonight.

Slowly, carefully casual, I went back along the little street. Then from the shadows of a doorway across the street stepped a dark form. I knew it was he. Actually, I'd had a feeling the whole time that he would stay in my vicinity. Or to be honest: I'd wanted just that.

He sauntered across the street to me. When he was standing close in front of me, he said politely, "Good evening," and held out his hand to me. I thought it was marvelous that he hadn't said, "Heil Hitler!"

I shook hands with him. And I sensed that he held my hand a little longer than was normal. His hand was larger and stronger than mine, but nevertheless he pressed it gently and almost tenderly, not with the bone-crushing grip usual among young men.

I answered shyly, "Hello." More than that I simply could not get out. I was afraid that my slight Polish accent would betray me.

"Why don't we have coffee together before everything closes?" he suggested. With joy I realized that his pronunciation also revealed a slight accent or dialect, but I couldn't place it for sure. From his appearance he didn't seem to come from north Germany, since he had rather dark skin and almost black hair.

I accepted his suggestion without hesitation. Together we walked back in the direction of the station and found a restaurant that was still open. While he gave the order, I looked at him more closely.

I judged him to be in his early or—at most—middle twenties, but when he laughed, he could have been seventeen too. Otherwise he was about the same size as I, but certainly stronger. I thought he wore the uniform of an airforce noncommissioned officer, but I really didn't know the insignia very well. A soldier in the German Wehrmacht—nothing could change that.

Except for the brief greeting, we'd exchanged scarcely a word. Finally the coffee came.

"Nice and hot, isn't it?"

Oh, if we could just have sat there quietly the whole evening! It really was enough just to look at him. But he was unrelenting.

"What's your name, then?"

"Stefan," I answered truthfully. An unrevealing name.

"Oh, just like my uncle in Vienna!" He nodded with understanding.

"Vienna?" escaped me rather unguardedly. So that's why the dialect.

"Yes, I'm Austrian. But of course today we all belong to the Pan-Germanic Reich. Where were you born?"

Now I was on the spot again. For the second time this evening, I put everything on the table.

"I was born here, in Toruń—and I am Polish. . . ." I was astonished myself at the clear voice in which I brought it out.

The young soldier looked around anxiously for a moment to see if anyone in the place had heard what I said. The fact that I'd used the Polish name of the city could, by itself, have caused trouble. But there weren't many people around at that hour. And the few there were seemed preoccupied. He asked softly, "But then you do have a night pass? I'm only asking because you can easily be arrested otherwise; you know that, don't you?"

This time I looked at him probingly. Yes, really, his voice sounded honestly concerned about me; there was no undertone of rejection or distancing that I could hear. Suddenly I realized that although I did possess the rotten pass, both of us were risking something if we continued to sit comfortably drinking our coffee. If there was a police roundup, he wouldn't come out of it unscathed either. Similar thoughts were undoubtedly going through his head. We both clutched our cups and stared into the distance for a few seconds.

Then, however, with a determined shake, he turned back to face me and said dryly, "Well, then—cheers, Stefan!"

And I, now in high spirits, answered, "Definitely, cheers—and what's your name?"

"Not a particularly original name—Willi. Just like my father and my grandfather. In our family we have no imagination in this department."

Before my eyes there arose a gallery of venerable Austrian ancestors with kaiser beards and stiff collars, and I had to laugh. What a good contrast the youngest Willi, with his youthful grin, was to them!

Now, for the first time, we attracted some attention. The barman stared over at us impassively. Probably he thought we were two late revelers who were trying to clear our heads with coffee. Shortly afterward he poked his finger at his wristwatch—just after midnight. By this time we were the only customers.

"Man, now I'm going to be late getting into the barracks," Willi moaned. But when he looked at me, his face softened again, and he added tenderly, "All because of you!"

"Thank you for the coffee," I answered sadly. I couldn't answer cheerfully anymore, because it was unimaginable that he would ever want to see me again.

It was all the same to me how late I got home. Mother and Mikolai were sound asleep, and my little sisters, too. So I decided to walk him to the station, where he'd try to get a taxi, because his unit was housed out beyond the two big city barracks. Silently we went the short distance across the station plaza. Just before he got in the taxi, he gave me his hand again. "Tell me, Stefan—when can we meet again?"

At first I couldn't believe my ears. "Excuse me?"

"I want to see you again—do you have time tomorrow evening?"

"Yes!" I said, and again, "Yes!" My heart was beating so hard that I gasped for air. "I'm finished at the theater at ten o'clock. Then I can wait for you here at the exit by the taxi stand!"

"I'll wait for you too!" he called to me through the rolled-down window as the car was driving away. I waved and jumped around in the snow like a clown. I was still waving when the car turned the corner and was out of sight. What an evening! What a meeting!

I took my time going home. I'd experienced so much, now I had to think about it all. I'd been looking for a friend exactly like that. Before my eyes I saw only him, this tender, handsome man—without his uniform, without the war and all of world history. Only him.

It wasn't until I'd quietly arrived home, undressed, and lain beside Mikolai on the floor that sad reality caught up with me again. What if my brother found out about Willi? What if one of his pals or one of Willi's superiors found out about us? It was impossible for us to just meet evening after evening in public.

So that was the first task. We had to find a hideaway. Some secret place just for us two. . . . Oh, we'd find something. Now that we'd found each other, the most difficult problem was solved: There was a man in the world who felt the same way I did. I fell asleep happier than I'd been in a long, long time.

In the next few days warmer weather set in, making the first snow melt. The temperature was more comfortable for running around outside at night, but some of the less-traveled side streets, which we naturally preferred so as to be able to talk undisturbed, turned into trenches of pure mud.

While Willi had less trouble with his military boots, I lost my only shoes the third night out. We were walking along one of the old country roads leading to the big highway east of the city that went from Lipno to Warsaw, when suddenly my right shoe stuck noiselessly in a mud hole.

As I carefully attempted to free it from the gooey mass, first the only buckle tore off, and then the heel remained stuck in the dark brown depths. In a rage I dashed the shabby remainder to the ground as well. Angry, helpless, and standing on one leg, I looked at Willi.

Without another word he grabbed me up and simply

carried me in his arms. He carried me over the largest of the mud holes that lay in front of us. Man, the last time that had happened to me was with Father, when I was four or five! Willi and I laughed as loudly and carelessly as if we were alone. As far as I was concerned, the rest of the world could consist of mud holes. . . .

After a while the path made an abrupt turn. Suddenly we were standing in front of a rundown old shed. It looked as if it hadn't been used for years.

Willi set me down directly in front of the weathered side door. The door gave at the first light push. We peered curiously inside. Willi tried to use his cigarette lighter, but it wouldn't catch. Luckily that night there was a full moon, whose pale light filtered down through some cracks and holes in the roof. Gradually we were able to get our bearings.

We rummaged through the entire shed, which did in fact seem abandoned but was still intact enough to make a fantastic hideaway. The total area wasn't very large—perhaps it had once stored animal feed. With our bare hands we set about clearing one corner of the dirt floor. Then we spread out a few boards we'd found.

Willi took off his heavy military coat and laid it over them. "Well, how do you like our private room?"

"First class, at the very least!" I answered with a giggle, and I threw myself down full-length on our canopied four-poster. Boisterously Willi pounced on me, and we scuffled around together as if it were a Sunday morning in Vienna, no war, no Occupation . . . as if we'd just woken up in Willi's bedroom in his family villa and afterward we would have breakfast with Father Willi and Grandfather Willi in the drawing room and would perhaps go riding for a while later, along the Danube if it was good weather.

"That's what you think!" he retorted. "Sunday breakfast at our house is the most boring experience of the whole week. The entire waxworks of our noble family is assembled then. And that's enough for the next seven days!"

I was amazed that he spoke of his family with such detachment. Until now I'd always listened openmouthed when he talked of all the possessions he'd obviously taken for granted all his life.

The memory of home turned him serious. Tenderly he laid his hand on my chest and came very close with his large, dark eyes. "Come, let's not talk of home. I'm much happier here with you."

With infinite tenderness, as I'd hardly been able to imagine with a man until now, he kissed me. He opened a few buttons of my shirt and let his finger glide carefully over my skin. I shivered. It was so different from the jerking off with the boys in the factory. And it was also different from that experience with Mikolai on my birthday. . . .

Afterward we remained clasped in each other's arms for a while. Our naked bodies were burning, and the cold outside only gradually penetrated to us. I sensed that the touching did him as much good as it did me and that we could give each other so much joy, as only two people can who . . . love each other!

Of course, that all sounds very romantic now, but I can say with utter certainty and without a doubt: This fellow in the German uniform, this tender man in my arms—he was my first great love!

For a long, silent moment Willi gazed piercingly at me. Then he whispered softly into my ear, "I've got it bad, Stefan! I want to live with you!" And after a while, "Just sweet words, huh?"

"No!" I contradicted him joyfully. "It's damned good. . . . It's damned strong!"

Imitating my Polish accent, Willi answered, "You've got it right, Stefan—it's good and strong for both of us! But damned, too!"

"But who's going to find out about it?" I replied with blind confidence. "Now we've just gotten a place where we can meet secretly. Just picture it—here every night at ten o'clock from now on. And there are no performances on Mondays, so I can come here from the factory right after work. . . ." As far as I was concerned, there were no more problems that we couldn't deal with.

Willi remained serious, however.

"Haven't you heard what the spirit is in Germany these days? Before, they say, you could be openly homosexual in the major cities. An older man in Vienna told me that he often traveled to Berlin in those days—that you could see men walking hand in hand on the street there. There were also a lot of clubs and organizations where boys and men could get together to fight for their rights. Can you imagine that?"

I shook my head. I'd never seen two men hand in hand on the street. And I pictured it as rather funny, but at the same time I thought—how stupid that there's not anywhere you can actually see men being tender with each other. Instead you see them drinking together, fighting together, there's even common masturbating, but basically that has nothing to do with tenderness. . . .

"Tell me more about those days!" I begged Willi.

"Well, it's too bad, but there's not much more to tell. In 1933 the Nazis banned all those organizations and closed most of the bars and meeting places. One of the most prominent leaders, a Berlin doctor who was both a Jew and a homosexual, was lucky enough to escape—he was traveling abroad and just didn't come back. But in the spring of 1933 they looted his institute and burned all the books and records. My old Vienna acquaintance told me all this—he used to visit this institute often."

"What happened to this doctor afterward?"

"I don't know."

"And what happened to the other homosexuals?"

"At first lots of them probably thought it wouldn't be so bad, since there were high-ranking Nazis who were known to be homosexuals. For instance the chief of staff of the SA, Ernst Röhm—everybody in Germany knew about him. But when he and his followers were suddenly bumped off in the summer of 1934, probably many people thought that things would get tough. And they did, too."

"But you're a soldier in the German Wehrmacht, after all," I said. "You're fighting for this Germany. How come you're so brutal to us Poles, to the Jews, obviously, to all kinds of other so-called subhuman people? You're a homosexual yourself, you yourself are a 'parasite on the people,' or whatever you call it—"

Willi sat up with a jolt. I'd hit him harder than I'd meant to. He gripped my arm. "Man, Stefan, don't go asking me such crap now! Yes, I think it's good that today there's a big, strong Germany again. I think this country is beautiful, and I'll always defend it. I can't help it if we also make some mistakes and errors. Your Polish government spoke out against the Jews before just as much as the Führer. It's just that he did what he said he would!"

Now I sat up too, swept his hand off my arm, and shot right back at him, "Oh, it's just an error when ten thousand of our men are simply mowed down by tanks and when hundreds of thousands of us are forced to do the filthiest work in your beautiful Germany? It was just an oversight that my father was carted off three years ago and my mother has scarcely enough to feed my sisters!"

My voice had grown loud and excited. "And you think that's a mistake—an error? Perhaps they'll err the next time about us two! Man, Willi, you're even more naive than I am!" It was as if my brother Mikolai were speaking through me. The words had just popped out. Now I couldn't take them back.

Willi slumped as I spoke. His shoulders drooping, the big fellow shook his head helplessly. "Damn it—what are we going to do about it?"

Now for the first time I felt older, yes, perhaps even a little stronger. All my anger evaporated instantly when I saw him sitting there so unhappily. Willi had understood what I was trying to say, and he was also trying to understand me. That was all I wanted.

We embraced and warmed ourselves. We would gladly have stayed there longer, but Willi absolutely could not be late getting back to his unit again. So we erased only the superficial traces of our sojourn but left the boards in place for our next meeting. Next time Willi would bring candles and something to drink.

Only as we were dressing did I remember my lost shoe. Willi gave me both of his thick wool socks. "At least you can get home with those. Tomorrow I'll try to organize a pair of boots for you!"

Unseen, we darted soundlessly out of our hideaway and ran along a good part of the way together on the old country road. We separated before we got to the city because there was a little shortcut to his unit's quarters at that point.

Soon after that I was home. Everyone was already asleep, as usual. How I would have liked to tell someone about my great happiness now. I loved and was loved in return. With a feeling of deep peace I closed my eyes.

WILLI DID IN fact bring me a pair of excellent leather boots on the following evening, and they just fit me. Now there began a wonderful period in which we furnished our small quarters ever more comfortably. After four weeks we had acquired a small spirit stove, some cans, blankets, and even a set of simple dishes. Where Willi got it all remained unclear to me. When asked, he was vague and evasive.

We'd managed to carve out a deep hole in one corner of the shed, exactly fitting a large wooden box nailed together from odds and ends of boards. This was our "vault," into which we stowed all our treasures before we left. Someone coming to the shed in the daytime wouldn't have been able to tell right off what secret meetings took place there daily,

or, rather, nightly. At home I said I had to work at the
theater even later. I explained the new, expensive boots and
other things that couldn't be bought anymore by saying that
I'd received them from German colleagues at the theater.

Mother was the only one who noticed a change in me.
Once she carefully inquired, "Stefan, boy—are all these
things really presents? Please don't get involved in something you might perhaps regret later. . . ."

"What do you mean, Mamushia?"

"I know you're an honest boy. But these days there's so
much illicit stuff going on, not only on the black market. I'm
just afraid you could get in with the wrong people. I know
you haven't stolen anything, maybe you were just taken in
by a crook. But the German police won't believe that. . . ."

I might perhaps have told Mother a bit more that evening
to reassure her, but unfortunately Mikolai was there. Too bad
he couldn't keep his comments to himself. "But my little
brother loves the Germans. Pavel told me that he was even
seen in the city last Monday with a German soldier. Report-
edly you were having a very nice conversation with each
other!"

Mother didn't go along with him. "Mikolai, why do you
say that? Stefan isn't a bad boy. Sooner or later we all have to
get along with the Germans somehow."

Mikolai glared at her. "If Father heard that! How can you
talk that way? I'll never accept the Germans' playing the
masters here. And Father wouldn't either!" With that he left
the room, slamming the door.

"He's so lonely," Mother wrung her hands helplessly, "and
he's right."

She cast a loving glance at me. "Why are you quarreling with each other so much all of a sudden? Please, Stefan, don't let yourself be seen on the street with soldiers. That comes back on all of us. And on Mikolai first, of course. You know how the other boys talk about something like that. . . ."

How I would have loved to tell her everything. But all I could think of was an evasive answer. "But soldiers aren't all the same, Mamushia. Most of them in the units moving up now are the same age as Mikolai."

Mother nodded, but she didn't say anything more. Had she perhaps for a long time known more than she let on?

PLANS
FOR THE
FUTURE

A NEW YEAR was about to begin—would it bring the long-desired end of the war? Would we perhaps at least get some news of Father finally?

On New Year's Eve, Willi and I were going to spend our first night together—a whole night of falling asleep and waking up! His unit was to receive two free days, and I'd told them at home that after the traditional performance of Strauss's *Fledermaus*, the theater would celebrate the arrival of 1942 there and so I'd spend the night with colleagues.

The first part was true, anyway. But immediately after taking off my makeup I had nothing more pressing to do than go to our shed. Willi was already waiting there. The little spirit stove was burning, and it was noticeably warmer here than outside, especially because we'd also set up a little lean-to in our corner that sheltered us from the larger overall space.

"You've come just in time, dear," he greeted me cheerily. "In a few minutes I'd have had to drink to our health all by myself!"

He'd brought a bottle of champagne and, as if that weren't enough, a couple of proper champagne glasses, too.

When he saw my astonished expression, he raised his hands reassuringly. "It's all right! Carefully swiped from the officers' club—my contribution to bracing the morale of the troops."

I'd never uncorked a champagne bottle by myself. "May I?" I asked him, and then carefully unwound the wire on the neck of the bottle.

A second later the cork shot out with a loud *pop!*—almost to the ceiling of our banquet hall. Thrilled, I watched it go. At the same moment a thick stream of the noble beverage bubbled out. I had trouble getting the foaming wellspring to flow into the tiny glasses.

"Just twelve o'clock!" cried Willi exuberantly. "You timed it exactly!"

"To a good year—with you!"

THAT NIGHT WE spoke about our futures for the first time.

"After the war I want to become a writer," Willi told me. "First I'd love to go to a university and study Germanic languages and literatures, and later write my own books and stories."

"You're lucky," I replied, not without envy. "I would so love to get proper voice training—but if you win, how will I ever have a chance to? Maybe I'll have to emigrate to America. I just thought of that recently, after I had another fight with my brother. I don't really know whether I have any future here. . . ."

"America?" Willi asked in astonishment. "But that wouldn't be good for me as a writer. It would surely take years before I could work in a foreign language. Perhaps we could both go to Ostmark—possibly we might be able to get you German citizenship through connections of my father's. Don't you at least have some German uncle or other, or, even better, a German grandfather in the family?"

If Mikolai heard that! Emigrating to America was bad enough. But to try to pass as German would have been complete betrayal in his eyes.

"Oh, if only the war would just be over," I said, determined to end our first, not exactly uncomplicated flight into the future.

"It doesn't look particularly good at the moment," Willi observed thoughtfully.

"For you?" I asked.

"Oh, at all. . . . We're completely stuck in Russia. No going forward and no going back. And then this stinking cold winter. I'm just hoping they don't rush us up from here as reinforcements. . . ."

I grabbed his hand, horrified. Oh God, I hadn't thought of that until now. Oh, not that. I'd even bury all my dreams of America immediately, if only Willi wouldn't be sent to the Eastern Front.

We calmed ourselves again and talked no more about it before we went to sleep, but a deep-seated unease lingered.

THEN, TWO DAYS before my seventeenth birthday, came the calamity with Mikolai. Again it was almost midnight when I softly opened the door to our apartment in order, as usual, not to wake anyone. To my astonishment there was still a light burning.

Mother was sitting beside her bed in the light of two candles. Since she had her back to me, I didn't at first see that she was bending concernedly over my big brother, who lay in the bed.

When I moved closer, she turned around and made a sign for me to be quiet. Her eyes were red with crying, and a few dark, disheveled strands of hair hung in her face.

"The Germans!" she whispered to me hoarsely, nodding toward Mikolai.

Good God—what had they done to him? Mikolai's face was pale and lifeless on the pillow. There were no signs of an external wound, but clearly something dreadful had happened to him.

Mother wiped his forehead with a cold cloth. Mikolai didn't react. I sat down on the floor beside Mother and took her hand. "What's wrong with Mikolai? You have to tell me what happened!"

"Not so loud, Stefan!" She tried to dampen my excited tone. "I don't know all that much either. Pavel and another boy brought him here two hours ago. Mikolai must have gone through something very bad—he seems to be in deep shock."

"But he's not wounded, is he?" Since he was covered, I was afraid he might have received an abdominal wound or something like that. Once I'd seen a soldier on a stretcher. He'd taken a shot in the belly and he'd looked just as pale and out of it as my brother did now.

For the first time Mother could reassure me of something. "No, he's not wounded, thank God. But a shock like this is no joke either. Just look—this great, strong fellow can't even talk. . . ." Again she cooled his forehead with a cloth dipped in cold water.

"Can I do anything for him or for you?"

Mother shook her head. "Not now, Stefan. I'm going to stay by his bed anyhow." Then, after a short pause: "It would be nice if you could come home earlier tomorrow night. I could be wrong, but perhaps your brother needs you now."

"I'll try to get a substitute for the stage tomorrow. Then I can be here right after the factory."

"Thanks, Stefan!" Mother looked at me so lovingly that I couldn't suppress a feeling of shame. It had been so hard for her since Father was taken away—and she'd never complained or let us feel her distress.

I had to swallow deeply a few times. Then I had an idea. "Do you think I could go over to Pavel's now? I have to find out exactly what happened to Mikolai."

"Yes," she said, nodding, "good idea! Run along—I was so horrified, I didn't get to ask very much, and then the boys were gone again. . . ."

Quickly I pulled on my warm jacket and ran along the next two blocks of apartment buildings to Pavel's family's.

UNFORTUNATELY ALL THE windows in the building were dark already. I walked through the unlocked front door into the entryway and tried to find some kind of a light switch. But I wasn't sure if there was one. Stumbling, I felt my way up the two flights to Pavel's apartment door. There wasn't a sound coming from inside.

I hesitated a moment. Then I knocked firmly on the wooden door—two times long, two times short. Not an especially original signal, but it should reassure them that no Germans were demanding entrance. We'd agreed to do it at the beginning of the war, and it had become a habit.

Still there was no movement. But Pavel must be home! He worked in the factory, as I did, and had to get up early. I knocked again.

Finally I heard shuffling steps. Then the door opened a crack. It was Pavel's mother.

"But Stefan—what's the matter with you? Why are you coming to us at this hour? We're all sleeping—Pavel too!"

"Please, let me talk to Pavel for a minute," I appealed to her. "I absolutely must speak with him. I'll leave again right away."

She mumbled something incomprehensible but finally opened the door and pointed to the end of the hall. "The boys are sleeping in there. But please be quiet and don't wake the others." And she disappeared without another word.

In the meantime my eyes had gotten used to the darkness. When I opened the door to Pavel's room, I first saw several boys lying scattered about on the floor, obviously more or less sunk in deep sleep. Then I caught sight of another one who wasn't asleep but was crouching at the window, staring over at me—Pavel! He'd recognized me immediately.

"Get out of here, you traitor!" he hissed softly at me before I could even open my mouth.

"Damn it all, you bigmouth!" I whispered back. "Come on out, I have to speak with you!"

He remained crouching at the window. "I have nothing to talk about with you. Get yourself out of here before I throw you out!"

Now I didn't care. Obviously I'd only get him out of there by provoking him the same way. "You stupid dog! Come out into the courtyard if you aren't a coward!" And with that I slammed the door to his room angrily and ran noisily down the stairs.

For a long time Pavel and some of the other boys in the factory hadn't deigned to look at me. Their rejection hadn't seemed important to me. But now it concerned Mikolai.

I stood alone in front of the door to the building for only a few minutes. Then I heard Pavel's steps on the stairs, and shortly after that the door was flung open. Pavel came up to me snorting with rage. Before I could say anything, he grabbed me by the neck and slapped me in the face with the flat of his hand.

With difficulty I wriggled out of his grasp. Pavel was somewhat older than Mikolai and just as strong. Despite the cold he'd only put on boots over his pajama bottoms and pulled on a somewhat tattered undershirt. Now he assumed the tense posture of a boxer. The muscles on his upper arms stood out clearly.

At first I was still trying to calm him. "Pavel, man, I'm here because of Mikolai. I have to know from you what happened!"

"You?" Pavel screamed at me, beside himself with rage. "You want to know that? You probably know better than any of us!"

And *whack*—I got another blow. There was really no

retreating now. Without hesitating further, I kicked him as hard as I could on his shin and then tried to punch him back. Hopeless—Pavel was in really good shape, and except for my one kick I never landed another blow. Pavel beat me up unhindered. I had the feeling that he was systematically taking me apart. Obviously he'd wanted to do this for a long time.

When I fell to the ground the first time, he even helped me up again. But only so that he could then land a last, comic-book-style punch on my nose. When I carefully lifted my head from the snow afterward, I saw that the heavy stream of blood from my swelling nose had colored the white ground red.

I sensed that Pavel was now standing over me. With my last strength I murmured in his direction, "What happened to Mikolai?"

Whether out of pity or some discomfiture over my persistence—finally Pavel flung me the information I'd wanted.

"Mikolai and two other fellows in our group were picked up by soldiers in the forest yesterday. The soldiers claimed they'd stolen weapons and hidden them. They let the two others go, but they stood your brother against a tree and said they'd shoot him if he didn't tell the hiding place."

Even Pavel had to catch his breath for a moment. Then he poked me lightly with his boot.

"Come on, stand up and stop pretending. If Mikolai wasn't your brother, we'd have taken care of you long ago. It's not good when someone plays the dandy and gets too chummy with the Germans. Now you see how your friends have treated your brother. . . ."

With an effort I dragged myself up from the snow. After a while I could stand almost upright in front of Pavel. "You heroic superpatriots make me puke!" I just couldn't keep from saying what I thought of him, though my cheeks had swollen, which made speaking somewhat difficult. "Where've you gotten so far by playing the daredevil? Nowhere, except now you can feel you're special and look down on other people. . . . Man, Pavel, I haven't squealed on Mikolai to anyone! The devil knows how you ran into that patrol. . . . But now, tell me, what did they do to my brother? He's lying there at home and he isn't responding to anything!"

Pavel looked at me seriously and, it seemed to me, search-ingly. He'd noticeably lost steam. In a quiet voice, for the first time, he said, "There was one of those German captains, a really brutal guy! We were lying behind some bushes not far away and could see everything that happened: They took off your brother's jacket and shirt and tied him to a tree. Then this captain began to scream, 'Where's the hiding place, Polish swine?' And since Mikolai didn't say anything, he fired a shot, just missing his head. It went on that way ten or fifteen times. At last the dog just yelled 'Polish swine!' and fired until his magazine was empty. . . .

"I don't know why he didn't kill him. Maybe he just didn't feel like it. Anyway, the captain went on with his people. They just left Mikolai tied to the tree, half-naked in the ice cold. . . . We waited a few minutes to see if they were really gone and then untied him. That's when we saw that his face was like carved stone and he wouldn't respond to anything. We even had to pull his jacket on like a little kid. When it was dark, we brought him to your house."

"Thanks, Pavel!" I said, before I turned and hurried back home. I saw his surprised look, but I didn't want to stand around with him any longer.

Before I got home, I tried to clean at least some of the blood off my face.

Nonetheless, Mother looked at my swollen nose with alarm and, guessing, asked, "Pavel?"

Mother and I huddled together beside Mikolai's bed. The stove had gone out ages ago. We spread a big blanket around our shoulders and sat there until morning. At some point, when it was getting light, she dozed for a little while, and I stood up and went without breakfast to work. Mikolai had slept quietly the whole night through.

DURING THE DAY I thought about who I could get as a substitute for the stage. Luckily I had only a relatively simple walk-on role in the current production. I thought first of Zygmund, a Polish stagehand who was just about my age and build; my costume would fit him without any alterations. Besides, he'd told me that for a long time he'd wanted to be on the stage and not just behind it. He agreed right away, and so we went to Herr Werner together.

"That's fine, Stefan," he said without hesitation. "Take the rest of the week off. You really don't look good."

Oh, yes, I hadn't even thought about my swollen face.

When I thanked him and was about to leave, Herr Werner added amiably, "Happy birthday, too—it is your birthday tomorrow, isn't it?"

I tried to smile. "Yes, my seventeenth!" I was glad he didn't ask me anything more.

I DIDN'T GO directly home from the theater, however. First I ran along the old country road to our shed to leave Willi a note. Along the edge of a piece of newspaper I wrote, without using any names:

> My brother was mistreated. I'm staying home for the next three nights to be there for him. I'll be back here on the fourth night.
> Love and kisses.

I fastened the paper to the board where Willi always hung his coat.

When I got home later, Mikolai was no better. In fact even somewhat worse, for he was running a high fever.

You could see by looking at her that Mother was completely exhausted. She'd sent my three little sisters to various neighbors so that Mikolai could have real quiet.

It was a good thing we could take turns caring for him over the next two days. There was really nothing to do, of course—except change his sweat-soaked shirt every few hours and now and then try to get some tea down him. But we both believed that deep in his subconscious he felt that someone was always near him.

Finally, on the third morning, I awakened Mother with good news before going to work: "Feel his forehead, Mamushia—the fever's gone! Mikolai's out of the woods!"

Mother leaped to her feet and felt his temperature and pulse. Then she leaned back, and both of us sobbed and cried with relief.

I ran to work almost gaily. Directly in front of the door to the factory, I nearly collided with Pavel. We'd both avoided each other since our fight.

"Mikolai's better!" I burst out.

Pavel showed no expression. Without a word he turned away to go to his section. After a few yards, however, he stopped and turned to me. "Say hello to him!"

I could scarcely wait for quitting time. When I finally got home in the afternoon, the sight was better than anything I'd hoped for: Mikolai was sitting up in bed and chewing on a piece of bread!

He was still very pale, of course, but he was grinning broadly. "Come here, you rascal—I've heard you had a fight with Pavel over me? Give him my regards, and tell him to just wait until I'm on my feet again. It'll be a long time before he's allowed to lay hands on anyone in our family!"

I was overjoyed that Mikolai was better. We both seemed to forget all the tension of the last few weeks. It had given way to a renewed feeling that we could rely on each other when it came down to it.

After days and nights of worry, there was finally a happy evening at home for us. My little sisters were also glad that we were all together again.

When Mother, exhausted by her long, sleepless nights, went to bed at the same time as the little ones, I sat down beside Mikolai's bed.

"Tell me, what day is today?" he asked suddenly.

When I told him, he looked at me, smiling. "That can't be! Then you just celebrated your seventeenth birthday without me?"

Oh, my birthday. Mother and I had completely forgotten it. The last one who'd thought about it had been Herr Werner.

Mikolai took my arm and pulled me close to him. Then this supermasculine man gave me a really tender kiss on the mouth and said, "Congratulations!"

All at once the experiences of that night with Mikolai a year ago appeared clearly before my eyes. I suddenly realized that perhaps there might never be another chance like this one to say everything straightforwardly.

"Mikolai, I have to tell you something that no other person in the world knows yet, not even Mother. It could be that afterward, when I've told you, you won't want to have anything more to do with me. But I can't help it. Either I can be your brother the way I am—or it all has no meaning anyway. . . ."

Mikolai let go of my arm and sat up. I sensed that he was ready to listen to whatever I had to tell him.

"You know what we did on my sixteenth birthday, when we drank together and you told me about girls. . . ."

He nodded and at the same time looked at me inquiringly. "Yes, and that wasn't bad, was it? You know how many boys do that together at our age! Hey, do you have a girlfriend?"

"Yes, something like that. A few weeks ago I met a German soldier, who's my friend."

Now it was out. Exhausted and relieved, I leaned back in my chair. Now whatever was going to happen could happen.

But Mikolai didn't get it at all. "Oh, you dull shit, why with a soldier? Man, if you have such a strong drive and can't find a girl, then do it with one of us—but why with a uniformed bully like that? You see how the dogs go after us when they're let off the leash."

Now I leaned over to Mikolai and looked him straight in the eye. "Man, I'm not talking about jerking off with a bunch of guys! I'm in love—please understand! I dream of men the way you do of women—and I love this soldier!"

I stared in fascination at the mute play of expressions on his face and waited to see which feeling would gain the upper hand: his scorn of "queers" and his friendship with the other boys who thought the same way he did—or his affection for me.

Finally his body relaxed a little. He wiped his forehead with the damp cloth and took a big swallow of tea. Then he spoke.

"I'm afraid for you, little brother! I'm afraid because hardly anyone will understand this, and I also don't know how I can explain it to any of our people. The funny thing is—all of a sudden I do understand you!

"To be honest, for the last few months I haven't understood. I was afraid you were taken in by all that stuff you were given by the Germans. I could never have forgiven you that.

"But what you tell me now—you know, I understand a whole lot more why you've held back from our crowd, and also why you've been at the theater so much. It's crazy, but I'm almost relieved to know that you were going around with the soldier not because you sold yourself as a traitor but because you—" It was still hard for him to find the correct word. "Love him?"

I nodded, silent and stirred. It had worked. He'd understood me. Without false pity, without superficial remarks about "queers." I felt that I didn't need to be afraid of the rest of the world now.

After this talk with Mikolai, an almost carefree period once again began for me, if you consider how very much everyone suffered under the general conditions of war. Rations for Poles had been reduced to a minimum, and there were no medical supplies at all. That problem was so much the worse because, ever more frequently, epidemics and infectious diseases broke out, which never would have occurred with better nutrition and adequate hygiene.

I'd reported to Willi in detail my talk with Mikolai. "A great guy, your brother!" he said appreciatively. "You know, I've also encountered bastards like that captain who tortured him. Usually they're basically unhappy people themselves. But you should never give any power to people like that, or it gets horrible, because they don't think anything of it if people suffer."

Then another thought came into my head that I'd wanted to ask Willi for a long time. "Does your father know that you'd rather be with men than with women?"

"Not at all!" He shook his head sadly. "He'd disinherit me at once."

I had to laugh. "You see, at least I don't have the problem with the inheritance."

FOR WILLI, THE WAR was something like a job, with working hours and time off. I, in turn, went to the factory. In the spring of 1942 there were hardly any activities that weren't "vital to the war effort." But the war itself, with its fighting and shooting, its murder and plundering, seemed far away from us, somewhere else—over in Russia or, now, down in North Africa. In our shed, about a mile from Toruń, now Thorn, there were only the two of us.

Then, one evening in the middle of April 1942, Willi burst into the shed and, without greeting me with his usual kiss, immediately said, "Man, Stefan—I've got to go to the front! The whole unit is being redeployed—we're moving out day after tomorrow."

My breath stopped. My hands began to tremble like mad. "Why—damn it? Why? Why?" I howled at him.

"Why?" Willi had only just found out that evening himself. "Why, you ask? Stefan—they don't give a shit whether we love each other or not! It's war!"

"What if you just desert? If we both try to make our way to someplace where there's no war?"

Willi looked at me pityingly. "And where's that? Where is there no war these days? We'd have to swim all the way to America."

"No!" I cried once more, trying to suppress the tears that were coming. It was horribly clear that we could do nothing about the approaching separation. The punishment for desertion was death.

It was the saddest evening I'd ever spent with Willi. First we considered how we would try to maintain contact through letters. Willi promised to write me at least every week, and as soon as he had a firm address, I could answer him there. In any case, I should wait for his first letter so he could send me his new field-post number. It was beyond question that we would not let anything separate us—not even this miserable war.

Naturally I was dreadfully anxious about him. Deployment to the Front—that meant an end to the comparatively comfortable service in the quartermaster's battalion. And—the risk of being killed! How many young men on all sides had already lost their lives in the fighting!

We stayed together until the last minute. It was uncertain whether his unit would get any more leave before they left. So we had to say everything important that night.

At last, to put off the parting a bit longer, I decided to accompany him almost to the main gate of his military quarters. We'd never done that before, for fear of being seen. Today we couldn't bother about that.

We embraced long and tenderly in a doorway near the camp. With the deep happiness we'd experienced in the past months, we no longer had any doubt that we wanted to spend our lives together.

IN THE FIRST few days without Willi, I managed to divert myself with additional work in the theater. When after two weeks there was still no letter from him, I became uneasy.

I no longer slept through the night but would wake up, plagued by anxious dreams of all sorts. I was glad that Mikolai now knew everything, and he responded with concern to my worries.

"Maybe he wrote to you long ago!" he said to me reassuringly one time. "You have no idea where he is now. It's possible that no mail goes from there at all. And then you'll suddenly get five letters at once."

Not one letter came to Toruń. Not in the first two weeks, not in the first month. After two months of waiting, I was so anxious that I would have done anything just to find out if he was still alive and in good health. Only how—how?

At the same time I had no doubt that he would write if he could. Except for Mikolai and Mother, I trusted no person in the world more.

It was already the middle of June when by accident I learned from Herr Werner that he sent letters to his brother, also on the Eastern Front, to a central military post office. From there the mail was forwarded to the actual military location through a field-post number indicating the particular section of the Front.

Once, after a rehearsal, when Herr Werner was called to the telephone for a moment, I secretly made a note of this address. It was clear to me what I had to do. There was little enough I could do. But I didn't want to leave that untried.

That very night I wrote to Willi.

THE
LETTER

IN THE MIDDLE of August 1942, I slipped the following lines into an envelope and sent them, firmly sealed, to the central Wehrmacht address for German soldiers at the Eastern Front:

Dear Willi!
 I haven't had any news at all of you for so long. I'm so worried about it. I miss you so much. I think of you every day. I am always thinking about you. I pray every day that you will come back safe.
 I'm working in the theater as before, but I'm not going out anywhere. Also not to the place we used to meet. I'm just true to you and will remain so for my whole life. Please write to me as quickly as possible so I can be reassured. I can't sleep, I think only of you.
 With love and kisses,
     Your Stefan

I considered for a moment whether I should put my return address on the back of the envelope, for Willi did have my address. But then I thought it would be sensible, because the letter might have to be sent back if it weren't deliverable.

Again the anxious weeks of waiting. Nothing happened. More and more often I had to think, Dear God, why didn't You protect him? I was still certain that he would have gotten in touch with me if it had been at all possible.

Meanwhile, at the theater, I began to work with the stagehands. I didn't enjoy wandering around the city any longer, because it just made me think of Willi all the more. During this period I became rather friendly with Zygmund, to whom I'd once poured out my heart because he was always very nice to me, and because I knew that he was also homosexual.

Everyone knew about Zygmund. Like me he had blond hair and moreover, to his distress, a really good growth of beard. While I admired a bristly beard and wished that mine would hurry up and sprout some more, Zygmund dreamed of going down in history as a diva, as he put it. When I first met him, I thought he was quite silly, running around backstage, made up and trailing long scarves. Involuntarily I thought, Typical queer—exactly the picture that Mikolai and his pals have.

But the more I got to know Zygmund, the more I thought, Really, why not? He's one of the most helpful, most cheerful people in the theater, and if it pleases him . . . ? Why do some people always have to tell other people what's good for them, anyhow?

My image of Zygmund changed one evening at the beginning of September 1942. We'd finished the last clearing up together and were just checking out with the stage doorman, each of us about to go home, when Zygmund poked me and asked, "Hey, romantic, are you still thinking about your big, strong dream man? I've really wanted to ask you for a long time if you could show me that shed you were telling me about."

I looked at him with raised eyebrows—why did he want to know that?

"No, little one, not what you're thinking!" Zygmund waved his arm dismissively. "I don't need any accommodations for my men. I just keep thinking about what you told me and thought we might perhaps see about clearing it out together sometime. What do you think?"

Really not a bad idea. Since Willi had left, I'd only been there a single time to fetch a few of our "treasures" and bring them home. I'd felt so terribly lonely there and so overwhelmed by all the memories that I hadn't been able to bring myself to go alone again. But with Zygmund, who knew at least roughly what I'd experienced, I was willing to risk it.

That evening the road seemed to me unusually long and difficult. Finally we reached the little rocky path. The view was blocked by the hill and the thick growth of trees, and like that very first night, the shed was not visible, although we were standing almost in front of it.

"This is it?" whispered Zygmund excitedly, looking around searchingly.

A moment later, when I leaned gently against the familiar side door to push it open, I felt a resistance. The door wouldn't open. Horrified, I looked at Zygmund—someone must have fastened the door!

Before we could summon up any further ideas, the door

suddenly flew open from inside and several men rushed out and collared us. Zygmund was still trying to get loose and yell, but he was simply lifted up by two fellows and dragged inside the shed. One of them held his palm pressed over Zygmund's mouth so he could only gurgle softly.

No sooner were we inside than one of them carefully fastened the door again and hissed softly at us in Polish, "Make one sound and you're done for! We aren't kidding!"

There could be no doubt about that. My eyes had gotten used to the dark, and I was able to make out four men all dressed in tattered prisoner's clothes. Their ages were hard to assess, because they were pitifully emaciated and unshaven. Three were certainly older than twenty; one was somewhat younger than Zygmund and I.

Zygmund was the first to speak. "Are you from Stutthof?"

What was he talking about? I was amazed at how calmly and deliberately Zygmund took over the discussion, although he'd just been hit in the face.

One of the men nodded. "And you're Poles from Toruń?"

Again Zygmund spoke. "Yes, don't worry, we won't turn you in. But there's a crowd of German military in the area— you know that, don't you?"

"We haven't much more to lose!" said the same man who'd spoken first.

"And where do you want to go from here?" Zygmund spoke as if he could suggest something.

One of the prisoners was still mistrustful. "What are we supposed to say to that? There aren't many alternatives for us. Can you help us with some food?"

Zygmund looked briefly at me. I nodded. I was definitely

ready to help. Then he said to the men, "There are four of you. That's bad. The way you look now, you can't let yourselves be seen anywhere. I'll make you a proposal: We'll give the boy with you some of our clothes. Then we'll take him into the city with us. I know people who have contact with the partisans. That's your only chance, if they get you out of here. Whether it will work, I don't know. But it's also too dangerous for us to come here with food. If anyone caught us with you, we'd be in just as deep—and it wouldn't help you, either. So—talk the idea over for a minute and let us know if you agree!"

My mouth dropped open: The everlastingly girlishly giggly Zygmund with his curled blond locks and dark-painted eyes was organizing a rescue operation that I could never have managed. While the men held a whispered conference, he poked me, grinning. "Now, don't look like that, little Prince Charming—what else could I do? D'you think they'd let us go alive if we didn't give them some hope of survival?"

For only a second I was afraid. "But you really mean it?"

Zygmund looked at me seriously and sadly. "I know that the Nazis in Germany routinely send homosexuals to vacation in their concentration camps: There's nothing in the world I'd rather do than to get one back on those barbarians." Only then did his roguish grin reappear.

Finally the first man, who spoke accent-free Polish, came back and crouched beside us. "Agreed—Pascal will go with you. He's just fifteen. A Jewish boy from Paris. He doesn't speak any Polish, but he does have a little German. Will that work?"

"We have to try it!" Zygmund nodded. "Let's not lose any

time now. The sooner you get in touch with the partisans, the better."

From Zygmund, Pascal got shoes and a scarf that he could wind around his prison uniform. I took off my shirt for him. Since it was a mild summer evening, it wouldn't attract attention that Zygmund now was barefoot and that I was shirtless. We looked like three friends who'd passed an evening out-of-doors and were now returning to the city.

Near where Zygmund lived we separated. "You shouldn't come along, Stefan," he said softly to me. "Some of our people still don't trust you. Don't take it wrong—there are wooden heads there, too! I'll tell you tomorrow at the theater how it all went."

I shook hands with them both briefly and then ran straight home. I couldn't help waking Mikolai and telling him in a whisper what had happened.

"Good!" he said when I'd finished. "That was the only right thing to do." And after a short pause he added, "Didn't you know that Zygmund's uncle is with the partisans?"

THE FOLLOWING EVENING, as soon as we got to the theater, Zygmund and I slipped away to the men's room to be able to talk undisturbed.

"Well, that boy was really very charming!" Zygmund began, with an absurd roll of his eyes. But then he immediately became serious and reported, "A friend of my uncle's went out during the night with Pascal. Apparently they got the other three men out of the shed this morning before dawn. But where they are now—no idea."

Zygmund and I seemed to have the same thought at the same time. I said, "We were there together almost every evening for months. Imagine if they'd showed up, or if we'd been discovered somehow. . . ."

"Yes, yes." Zygmund was already grinning again. "You see, sometimes 'Love makes you blind!' " He laughed joyously at his own joke. "Incidentally, we shouldn't be seen anywhere near the shed anymore. The military patrols looking for the escapees might still stumble on the hideout."

I never saw the shed again.

IT WAS EXACTLY one week later, during work at the factory—September 19, 1942. I will never forget the date. I was standing sunk in thought at my place, repairing old hoses, when the voice of my foreman jolted me: "Hey, Stefan—are you asleep? You have to go see the boss at once!"

I? What was that supposed to mean? I'd only ever seen the boss from a distance, and I'd never exchanged a word with him.

Carefully I washed my oily hands clean, then went over to the offices to knock on his secretary's door. She sent me right through. "Herr Krieger is waiting!"

He had his back turned toward me when I entered and was still on the telephone. In a minute he hung up the receiver and turned to me. "Stefan?"

I nodded dumbly.

"Pack up your things!" he said in a curiously matter-of-fact manner. "That was the Gestapo. They want to ask you about something. Have you been involved in anything illegal?"

Gestapo—the German secret police. What could they want with me? Suddenly thoughts of the shed shot through my head: Had we left behind any clues? Had the escapees been caught and betrayed us out of fear or despair?

"Should I go now, Herr Krieger?"

"Yes, at once. What do you think?" he growled back.

Apprehensively I packed my little satchel. I hadn't even eaten my morning bread yet.

The Gestapo had set up their headquarters in the former villa of a Jewish doctor. The doctor had been taken away with his entire family at the beginning of the war. Two German policemen patrolled in front of the gate of the estate. I told them that I'd received a telephoned summons. They patted down my jacket and trousers for weapons before letting me go unaccompanied to the entrance of the house. There a plainclothesman took down my personal data, telephoned briefly, then took me to a room in the basement of the house.

A brief knock, then he opened the door and shoved me into the room. He shut the door softly behind me and was gone.

Opposite me sat a slender, fortyish man in uniform behind an immense desk. The room itself was not very large, and there was an adjoining room that appeared to be sparsely furnished. I didn't move from the spot.

He looked up from his file folder, firmly ground out a cigarette half-burned at the most, and looked me over at length. Then, without any greeting, he shot out a few questions: "Name?" "Date of birth?" "Domicile?"

I answered each one as clearly as I could. But still he interrupted twice to bellow, "Louder!"

I continued to be unable to figure out what he really wanted from me. Suddenly he waved me forward a little with his forefinger. I took two timid steps forward.

He sifted through a few papers in his file folder and finally pulled out a small brown note, which he slapped on the desk directly under my nose. "Do you recognize this letter?"

The brown note—my God. . . . My heart thundered so loudly in my ears that I thought I'd have to scream to get out an answer at all. But nothing happened—no sound escaped my lips. Before me lay the letter that I had written to Willi almost two months before.

"Did you write it or didn't you?" The voice of the uniformed man was sharp and commanding.

I nodded dumbly. I began, very slowly, to comprehend the whole reality. Some person must have opened the letter and betrayed us, probably to a superior. Or had they found the letter on Willi when he was wounded or perhaps even killed?

The first words that I haltingly got out were "What's wrong with Willi? How is he?"

The officer leaned back, confirmed. "So, you did write to him!"

I was in danger of losing control completely. "Please, I beg of you—just tell me if he's alive and if he's all right!" In my agitation I'd moved a step toward him.

Instantly he raised his hand and slapped me resoundingly in the face: "Back, you homo rat!"

I tottered to the door and endeavored to stand up straight

somehow. I would do anything if only he'd let me know what had happened to Willi.

The man said nothing at all for the time being but pulled a typewriter toward him in a very businesslike manner and rolled a form into it. While he rolled in the sheet, I could see very clearly the black lettering at the top of the paper: WARRANT OF ARREST.

"So then, you admit that you wrote this letter in your own hand and sent it?" he began almost in a monotone.

Why should I lie? I admitted that I'd written the letter to Willi because I was very concerned about him. He'd been a good friend to me, and we'd met a few times in the city near the railroad station. Naturally I said not a word about the shed.

"Did you have sexual intercourse with each other?" he asked in exactly the same monotone.

From his mouth the words sounded so nasty that I answered with a clean conscience, "No!" We'd loved each other more than once—but what would this fellow know about that?

I feared that he sensed something of my scorn, for suddenly he looked up coolly and said to me, "You take me for your fairy godfather, don't you? Wait awhile, queer boy, there's a surprise in store for you. . . ."

Without wasting another glance on me, he pecked out half a page more on the form and pulled it out with a jerk. "Sign here!"

I tried to at least skim the lines, but then he yelled again, "Sign, damn it!"

Without hesitating any longer, I signed. As far as I'd been able to read, it was even correct. Almost in the middle I'd been able to decipher "The detainee refuses to admit that he practiced sexual intercourse with the Army member. . . ."

He dialed a telephone number, and a moment later a young soldier entered to lead me away. When we were already in the doorway I turned once again. "Do you know anything about how Willi is?"

He took no notice of me. He only gave the soldier a slight wink. "Out!"

For the rest of the day I was locked in a solitary cell—that is, a cellar room furnished as a prison cell, with a coverless folding bed, a pail, and a tiny window. First I'd had to give up my belt and my shoelaces and empty all my pockets.

Hour after hour I sat alone in the cell. Sometimes I could hear bootsteps outside, occasionally a bellowed order, otherwise nothing. I felt no hunger and no thirst. But my anxiety about Willi tortured me.

Later, toward evening, I began thinking painfully of Mother, Mikolai, and my little sisters. What must Mother have suffered when she was informed that her son had been arrested by the Gestapo? And what would Mikolai think— and what would he tell his buddies?

As long as it stayed light, my mind remained relatively clear. When it was dark and I continued to have no idea what was going to happen, real panic overwhelmed me. Perhaps nothing had happened to Willi in the fighting. . . . Perhaps my letter had delivered him to the Gestapo. . . . Someone or other at the theater had once said that homosexuality in the

SS, the military, and the police was punishable by death. . . .
I'd dismissed it as a horror story.

Thoughts revolved in my head. I crouched in one corner
of the room without rightly knowing where I was. The whole
thing was like an unending nightmare from which I hoped to
to be awakened.

But there was no such release. When it began to grow
light outside, I was still sitting in the same corner, my eyes
wide open. A hatch in the door clattered down, and in it
appeared a piece of bread and a tin bowl of some warm, dark
water.

My legs were asleep from being cramped in one position
for so long. But the pain helped me to slowly find my way
back to the reality of the miserable little cell. This was no
nightmare. I'd been arrested because of my love letter to
Willi, and at the moment it was impossible to see what was
going to happen next. At least I could pee in the bucket and
choke down the moldy bread. I made up my mind not to
disgrace our love.

Soon I heard steps approaching the door. Two guards put
me between them and took me down the corridor, to a room
that looked exactly like the side room I'd seen at my first
interrogation: a plain stone floor, white-painted walls, a
wooden table, three or four simple chairs, and on the wall a
faucet and drain.

The two guards, whose uniforms I could not identify,
ordered me to take a position at the wall opposite the table
and to wait. Then they slammed the door shut from the
outside. I had been standing there for a few minutes at most
when the door flew open again and three men came in, of

whom two were in shirtsleeves and the third wore an officer's uniform with the insignia of the SS. This one had under his arm the folder I'd seen the day before.

The two younger men sat on the chairs and gazed straight ahead in a rather bored way. The officer shifted a chair forward, turned on a desk lamp, and spread the file out on the desk.

"Heil Hitler!" he greeted me, as if we'd arranged to meet here.

Politely I answered "Heil Hitler!" but was not so foolish as to add anything else.

The man assumed an air that was downright affable. "No big thing, is it?" he offered, without looking up from the file, "in any case not for you. You're seventeen? Well, I advise you to admit everything honestly, that's the best way for you to get out of here!"

He then repeated the questions I'd already answered the day before. His questions were polite, at times almost interested, at least always matter-of-fact.

At the place about sexual intercourse he stopped briefly and looked at me for the first time. "But you loved each other, didn't you? Man, two such young boys without women. . . ."

With unbelievable naïveté I nodded almost proudly. "Yes, we loved each other very much!"

He made a few notes for himself and then pulled a few other papers out of the folder. "So—that's that. Now we'll really get down to business!"

I couldn't begin to imagine where he was heading and looked almost curiously at the photographs and papers he arranged in front of him. In a friendly manner he waved me forward. "Yes, take a chair and sit down here!"

I still didn't suspect anything. The two young louts continued to look around in boredom.

From the pile of photographs he pulled out two. "Here, take a look: These are the sort of fellows who've often approached boys, some of whom were much younger than you. These two here are from Thorn—you certainly know them, don't you?"

I'd never seen either man in my life. I shook my head. He looked up briefly. His facial expression perceptibly cooled. But he continued to root around in his photos.

"And this one here?"

I had to say no again.

"And here—this one here?"

I hadn't enough control over myself yet to conceal a slight wince. That was the first man that I actually recognized— the young tenor from our theater who'd so marvelously played the Gypsy baron Barinkay. How on earth should I react?

"And?" All friendliness suddenly fell away from the man.

Still I didn't dare react. Unexpectedly, he pushed me off the chair and sprang to his feet. "Now, that's the end of the kiddie performance! These were all notorious queers from Thorn—don't think you can play the innocent here. I need your statement to put these criminals—these seducers of youth—out of business, and if you try to get out of it, you'll get it in the neck too, you little hooker!"

He'd bellowed himself into a rage. I was again standing stiffly in the spot where I'd been at the beginning of the interrogation and said not a word. He gave a wave of the hand to the two louts and sat back down on his chair. They stood up and placed themselves directly behind me.

"So—once again!" The SS officer brushed something from his sleeve and took up the photos. "Who is that?"

"I really don't know," I said softly.

He only slightly raised his eyebrows, and immediately one of the thugs punched me in the side. It hurt dreadfully when I breathed, but I remained standing stiffly in my place without wavering.

"Where did you have it off with this one here?" he screamed, and poked his finger at the picture of the young tenor.

"I only recognized him from the theater," I replied quickly, before one of the two behind me could let go again.

"So, you won't cooperate with me? All right!" His voice suddenly became so soft again that I could scarcely understand him. "I'll leave you alone for a bit with my two friends here. Perhaps you'll recollect something afterward." He packed his pictures and files together and left the room, closing the door softly and properly behind him. I was about to long for the return of this offensive fellow.

He'd scarcely left the room when one of the two shoved me over against the table again. In bad German he bawled at me, "Take off your pants, you assfucker!"

I clutched the table with both hands and did nothing. What could I do against two professional toughs? My only hope was that it might pass quickly.

As both came at me, they removed the leather belts of their trousers.

"I never repeat my orders!" the first one now said arrogantly, stopping right in front of me. As I carefully lifted my head to look him in the eye, the first blow of his belt hit me so hard in the face that the skin on my forehead burst open and blood began to run down one side of my face.

"I can only advise you to take down your pants, you Polish swine of a queer, if you don't want to look damned ugly for the rest of your life!" he shouted at me sneeringly, and let his belt whip into my face a second time.

With trembling fingers I tried to open the buttons of my trousers. A third blow hit me on the back.

Now the second one began to join in. "Does it always take you so long, asshole?"

Finally I slipped off my long black trousers. Again a blow hit me.

"Go on, go on, the underpants too, and then put yourself all nice over the table on your belly!"

For the first time I began to shake. My knees trembled terribly, and it was simply impossible for me to remove my underpants without falling down. The two of them seemed to find watching me amusing, for as long as I was struggling with those damned underpants they stopped and watched me intently. At last one of them ripped away the pants with a jerk and pushed me hard against the table.

Until this point I had never in my life known how much pain a human being can endure before he is no longer a human being, before pain causes him to lose all sense of time and place and finally consciousness altogether. Of the following hours and days I remember only the dull quaking of my flayed body whenever I was thrown somewhere or was stood up again and fetched. The scale of the pain no longer changed perceptibly. Everything hurt unceasingly.

From shoulders to thighs I was wounded, raw, bleeding flesh. The only thing I could do to orient myself was to somehow make sure I was lying on my stomach when a torture session ended and I was thrown back into the cell. At last I no longer clearly understood why I was there at all. Willi, Mother, and Mikolai—they were no longer present in my world. . . .

After some days—how many exactly I couldn't say—I was left lying for longer periods. Earlier I'd received only tea or water every once in a while. Now I was given a sort of broth, which one of the other prisoners tried to feed to me.

In between beatings I would fall into a light sleep, but after a short time it would be shattered by frightful dreams in which all the scenes of the previous days happened over and over. At last I had such a fear of sleeping that I used much strength trying to remain awake as long as possible.

Eventually the beatings ended, and after two days I could stand up again by myself and use my pail. My wounds were untreated and burned and itched terribly. Except for the pail and the bed, I had only a hard horse blanket.

Around this time my things were thrown in to me. I put them on slowly and carefully, so as not to reopen the newly scabbed-over wounds. That same evening I was fetched and taken to a new interrogation. My whole body was trembling, because I feared the beating was going to start all over again.

It's almost impossible to imagine that I was actually

relieved when I again saw the SS officer who'd showed me the photographs at the beginning. He appeared busy with something else and looked up, slightly disturbed, when the guard delivered me to his office.

"So—everything all right? This is our deposition, which you have to sign here."

I didn't dare ask whether I would then be free, or what was written in the many pages of text. I only said, "Yes, I'll sign it!" and with trembling hand put my name at the bottom of the document.

As I signed, I was at least able to make out the date: I'd been there twelve days!

Immediately after signing, I was handcuffed, and a guard took me to one of the trucks with gratings standing in front of Gestapo Headquarters. Another, apparently older prisoner was transported with me. He didn't look very good either, and he stared fixedly into space during the entire trip.

Peering through the grated window from time to time, I soon knew where the ride was taking us—to Okraglak, the old Round City Prison of Toruń. At least there I'd be out of the talons of the Gestapo.

At Okraglak an older clerk informed me that at the moment there were no special prison uniforms. I would have to keep on my own quite filthy civilian clothes at first, and then write to my mother so she could bring me laundry for a change. Before I was locked into a group cell, he led me to a photographer, who took three pictures of me as a prisoner awaiting trial.

Although I had to spend almost three months in the

group cell with between eight and ten other prisoners, I have
scarcely any memory of it. At the beginning I thought they
must all be big-time criminals, as they looked so tattered and
battered. But when after a few days I was led to the shower
for the first time and happened to pass a mirror, I discovered
with shock that my appearance wasn't much better. Like
most of them, I was quiet and turned in on myself. Everyone
was waiting fearfully for his trial and whatever fate it would
bring him.

During the whole time I wasn't allowed to write a letter
home. Twice I was allowed merely to fill out a form for things
that I wanted. Mother and Mikolai were also not allowed to
write to me. Visitors were strictly forbidden. Some items of
clothing that Mother had sent in to me I traded shortly
afterward to another prisoner who had almost nothing to
wear and who gave me some of his bread for them. My
hunger grew worse the longer I was there.

One afternoon it began to snow lightly, and as I did so
often, I was staring out of the cell window, from which I
could catch a glimpse of a tiny piece of the street in front of
the prison. Suddenly I didn't dare believe my eyes: Wasn't
that Mother who had walked slowly past?

As loudly as I could, I bellowed, "Mamushia!" through the
bars. Before I could repeat my cry, one of my fellow prisoners
tore me away from the tiny window and threatened me with
his fist. "Pipe down, little one! D'you think we want to get
into trouble because of you and your mama?"

It was strictly forbidden to call out from the cell block. Of
course, I'd completely forgotten that at the moment. Nevertheless I clung tightly to the bars again to perhaps catch

another glimpse of Mother. And sure enough, there she came into my sight a second time and looked searchingly up at the high wall with the tiny windows—ah, dear, dear Mamushia! For over an hour I stared through the bars and three more times saw her go along the little piece of street that I could make out. Then I didn't see her anymore. My fingers were numb from the ice-cold bars. Directly under the window I sank to the floor and wept bitterly. The tears came from the depths of my soul, where even the Gestapo's beatings had not been able to reach. . . .

IN DECEMBER 1942, a few weeks before my eighteenth birthday, I was suddenly informed one morning that my trial would take place that same afternoon. I had to shower and put on my last pieces of clean clothing. Afterward I wasn't allowed back to the group cell. Toward midday the prison truck collected me and delivered me directly to the court. I waited for about two hours in a small room and then was led from there straight into the courtroom.

The large wood-paneled hall was virtually empty. At the front sat three men in dark robes along with a fourth, younger man, who obviously was going to record the proceedings. I was directed to a chair a few yards from the judges. Now for the first time I dared to look around briefly and to cast a glance into the spectator area. There alone in the first row, proud and erect, sat a woman in dark clothes—Mamushia! She cast a hardly noticeable smile at me. My God, what was she going to have to listen to here!

After the reading of some general personal information about me, the middle of the three men opened the "questioning." I wasn't really asked anything more at all—the judge contented himself with presenting his view of the matter without once allowing me to say two words in a row.

"The accused," as he began every other one of his high-flown sentences, "has committed sodomy repeatedly and with various partners of the male sex, and without the development of even a rudimentary comprehension of the reprehensibility of his acts. And this, furthermore, is not merely a recent occurrence but one that has continued for at least one to two years. The accused, a Pole by birth, has not only practiced this disgusting act with those of his own kind but has also not been deterred from committing it with members of the German Wehrmacht as well. And this he has admitted in at least one case. Thus I plead in accordance with Paragraph 175 and 175a of the German penal code for a sentence of several years of incarceration, in order to isolate the accused from society and give him the opportunity to become a human being again."

I'd hardly understood half of his inflated words. What must Mother be thinking?

A few minutes later the sentence was read: "Because of the seriousness of the offense, the accused is, despite his youth, sentenced to five years in prison!" Without once looking at me, the judges clapped their file folders shut and the clerk stuffed his papers into a briefcase.

A guard gripped me by the arm and led me out of the courtroom, passing not far from Mother. We weren't allowed to exchange a single word. When I tried to slow my pace, the guard pulled me along impatiently. I had one last view of Mother—she was standing erect, looking toward me. She tried another smile, and both of us had silent tears running down our cheeks.

PRISON

TWO OR THREE days after the trial I was sent in a convoy to to the notorious prison of Koronowo, then known by its German name, Crone. Even before the German Occupation it had had a fearsome reputation. Now only Poles and Polish Jews were serving time there. All German prisoners had been released or transferred. Some of the Polish and Jewish inmates had been there since before the war; some, like me, were newly incarcerated under German laws.

Koronowo was hell. The guards supervised only our work duties; the rest of the time the rule of fist governed: Only those who were strong could hold their own. Directly after my arrival, my civilian clothes were taken away and my head shaved bald. Before I received worn and torn prison clothing, my entire body was dusted with a nasty, stinking disinfectant.

Then I was shoved into a block that consisted of gigantic communal cells. Actually, the cells weren't so large, but at times there were some forty men housed in each cell. The cell door was hardly banged shut behind me when all eyes were turned toward me. Immediately a youth not much older than I kicked me in the behind in greeting, so that I stumbled three or four steps into the middle of the room.

"Hiya, assfucker!" he bawled derisively.

Luckily the others barely listened to him. An older and amazingly sturdy prisoner waved me over to him.

"Watch out, queer! Here, I'm the boss. That means I and my people give the orders. We're lifers, whereas with luck you'll be outside again in a few years. Listen carefully: We control the food here. If you ever dare hide something away for yourself without asking us first, we'll make you suffer. There are no more beds free here. Watch out where you roost!"

With that he turned back to one of his pals. The interest of the others also waned. They'd briefly checked to see if anything spectacular was to occur, but the entrance of a Polish boy who'd been sentenced under Paragraph 175 obviously wasn't very extraordinary. A welcome like that seemed to be normal here.

I looked around uncertainly. Where could I settle for the night without immediately stirring up trouble again? There was a horrible stench in the cell. Now I discovered the source: In one corner of the room stood a few buckets for calls of nature, which were obviously emptied only infrequently. In the opposite corner, in the neighborhood of a tiny round iron stove, the boss and his people had established themselves. I tried to slip in somewhere along the edge.

All this time the youth by the entrance hadn't let me out

of his sight. Now he came up to me again. "Get away from here! That's my place there. You think I want to be mauled by an assfucker all the time?"

I'd have loved to clip him one on the spot. What did this bigmouth think? Weren't all of us here in a damned miserable situation? I suppressed the impulse. I wanted to understand exactly what the rules here were first. Without wasting a glance on him, I went along a few yards farther and sat on the floor beside a skinny older man who was trying to repair his split shoes.

I looked at him inquiringly. He nodded slightly and then turned again to his shoes. The floor was ice cold. How was I going to sleep there without getting pneumonia the first night? The old man noticed my searching look and with a quick wave of his hand pointed under the nearest bunk. There was some filthy hay there. I managed clumsily to pull a few bundles out and tried to make myself something like a bed in the last tiny free space.

Soon after that the boss bellowed some kind of order, which I didn't understand. In a rush the men lined up to pee, right there in front of everyone, into the buckets. I didn't find out until later that a brief visit to the toilets was permitted only once a day, in the mornings before work. The procedure was mostly over when suddenly the single naked light bulb in the room went out. All the men took up their sleeping places amid murmuring and grumbling.

After only a few minutes, to my horror, I became aware of itching and tickling all over my body. Since it was too dark to be able to see anything, I tried to feel with my hands—ah, how horrible! The straw was infested with all kinds of vermin, which were entirely unfazed by the hefty dose of disinfectant I'd received. And the fleas and lice and I-don't-know-what-else were so small that you couldn't just brush them off. In some cases they'd already fastened themselves onto my skin. When I succeeded in brushing some off, others immediately appeared to take their place—and even worse: The next morning all over my body were little red inflamed spots where I'd torn off the bodies of the little devils, the legs or suckers still stuck in my flesh. Sleep was almost out of the question.

Suddenly—in the middle of the night it seemed to me, for it was still dark—a shrill whistle blew close by. Everyone around me sprang up. Each one tried to get to the door first. The old man beside me shook me, but in a comradely way, and growled, "Get up now, youngster. We only have five minutes to use the toilets. Five minutes for forty adult men. . . . The rest of the day you can crap in your pants. So come on now. . . ." And with that he stumbled after the others.

I felt so exhausted that I sat looking around for a moment. What sort of a world had I gotten into! The single light bulb came on again. The cell was empty except for the boss, who had given the whistled command, and two of his henchmen, who obviously weren't required to participate in group shit-ting. And wasn't there someone else, too? Sure enough—out of the boss's bunk, drunk with sleep and clad only in underpants, clambered the youth who yesterday had tried to make me look ridiculous in front of everyone. Our glances met for only a second. No one said a word. I acted as if I thought nothing about it and trotted toward the door after the others.

But I was too late. The others were already coming back, hastening to their sleeping places to get out tin plates and dented cans, and lining up near the boss.

"You, stay here!" our chief commanded me as I was about to leave the cell. I looked inquiringly toward him.

"You take away the piss buckets!" To my neighbor, the thin old man, he gave the order, "Go on, show the new one where it is and take the other two pails yourself!"

Silently we snatched up the stinking slop pails. The wretched things were terribly heavy. And it wasn't at all easy to walk so steadily that they didn't keep spilling over. When we finally got to the big latrine and had tipped the stuff out, I noticed that the old man's whole body was trembling. We both stank to high heaven.

Suddenly he grasped my hand and gasped out between panting breaths, "I'm Keitelberg, the Jewish tailor Keitelberg—have you ever heard of our firm in Warsaw?"

Shocked, I shook my head. What had this man been through already? What was still in store for me?

"You know, I have a boy, that is, I actually have four boys and two girls, but I have one boy who must be just about the same age as you. I haven't seen any of them at all for months. . . ."

He was still clasping my hand. "You've got to survive all this here, you hear? I know I'm not going to manage it much longer, but you have to hold out, promise me? There must be people who someday can tell what's happening here. . . ."

I still didn't know how to answer him. But his words struck me deeply, and for a moment I forgot my own misery, all the itchy places on my skin, my painful hunger, and my longing for Willi, Mother, and Mikolai.

"Can I do anything for you?" I finally stammered awkwardly.

Then at last he let go of my hand. "Yes, boy, go to the toilet quickly now before we have to go back!" He attempted a smile and I darted to the latrine.

When we got back to the cell, the apportioning of some sort of warm fluid into the tin bowls was already in full swing. Since I had no container for the broth, the old man declared that we would both use his pot. He actually did manage to get somewhat more poured into it.

Meanwhile a gray day had begun to dawn. We lined up for roll call and were marched to our various work areas. On this morning I learned how monotonous it is to unwind old sisal rope. It was to remain my sole activity in all the following days, weeks, and months. Ten hours per day, six days a week. In between we were sent out once daily for an hour in the fresh air and had to rush around a muddy field at a run. Anyone who stumbled was hit in the back with a club or a whip. Once, when I lost one of my heavy wooden shoes, I received such a terrible blow across the kidneys that for a week I could scarcely breathe. But that wasn't anything unusual in Koronowo. It was almost commonplace.

Besides, the rumor circulating among us prisoners was that it was much worse in the quarries at the Sachsenhausen concentration camp. Since more and more reinforcements were needed for their labor gangs, we anxiously asked ourselves which of us might be the next ones to be transferred there. Herr Keitelberg had told me once that many homosexuals were interned and tormented there in particular. This man always looked after me and now and again even slipped me some of his bread. At first I absolutely refused to take it, but then he would always say, "My stomach just won't stand anymore. Please, you eat it, Stefan, before the boss and his gang grab it."

In 1943, my eighteenth year, the spring, summer, and fall passed without my taking any real notice of the wonderful change of seasons that used to give me so much pleasure. Like many other prisoners, I'd developed a chronic cough from the fine sisal dust, which settled in the mucous membranes of the lungs.

Every two months each prisoner was allowed to write a letter home. Under one condition, however: The letters had to be couched in correct German, so they could be read by the supervisors. Only a few inmates could write the least bit of German, let alone without mistakes. Herr Keitelberg saw that it was an opportunity for me: "Stefan, offer to help the others. Every talent you can dredge up here helps you survive!"

A few days later I hesitantly volunteered to the boss, who didn't know correct German himself. I said that I was ready to help with letter writing.

He looked at me mistrustfully. "For how much?"

What did he mean by that? Herr Keitelberg boldly called out, "For the usual rate! Two per letter!"

"Okay!" The boss nodded. "Here, show what you can do!"

Thus began my career as a prison scribe, which I owed

entirely to old Keitelberg. I received the usual prison currency unit of two cigarettes per letter, which, since I didn't smoke and anyway there was never enough tobacco in circulation, was paid in food. To this day I wonder why the gang around the boss never stole back what they had given me, whereas they commonly did so with the much smaller mealtime rations.

If someone was almost starved to death, I wrote the letters for nothing. Of course, I have to acknowledge that I did this only if Herr Keitelberg and I weren't exactly faint with hunger. Today I'm ashamed, but at that time I simply couldn't summon up the greatness to go without just because someone else was also suffering from hunger.

Nevertheless, my standing rose remarkably during this period. The vulgarities about my homosexuality grew rarer. Perhaps the men even respected the way old Herr Keitelberg and I stuck by each other—though there was no sexual relationship between us—unlike some of the others, who still cheated each other whenever they could.

At the end of 1943, one evening a German guard appeared and ordered our cell boss to the door. The two whispered together for a moment while we others anxiously put our heads together. Were there still a few men needed for the next convoy to Sachsenhausen? Then our chief was bellowing in my direction: "Stefan—come here! You've been chosen for a special duty! Get going!"

My heart stopped. This was the end! Herr Keitelberg, too, became quite pale with fright. The others looked rather relieved. However, no one gloated over my bad luck. At the last moment, I gave Herr Keitelberg my remaining cache of cigarettes and bread and then crept along behind the guard. Herr Keitelberg looked as numb as if he himself were being led to execution.

We were barely outside when the guard said to me, "Why aren't you glad? There's a place open in the writing room. They need someone there who can speak and write German. You can, can't you?"

Still nearly paralyzed with fear, I couldn't react at all at first. And yet of course I knew that working in one of the offices or rooms was linked with all sorts of privileges. That very day, for the first time since I'd been in Koronowo, I was allowed to take a warm shower; I was disinfected a second time and received a prison uniform that, although mended many times, was nevertheless clean. What a pleasant feeling on the skin! From then on I was housed in a three-man room. Next morning early I intended to take the good news to Herr Keitelberg.

But all the men were already off to work when I quickly ran over to our old communal cell the next morning. The work in the writing room was incomparably easier and pleasanter than unraveling that filthy sisal.

In the evening, before the night roll call, I was finally able to get over to the old cell. The men greeted me in an almost friendly manner and congratulated me on my promotion. Nevertheless, there was a peculiar tension in the room that I didn't know how to interpret right away. When I turned my eyes to Herr Keitelberg's place, the spot was empty. My God, where was he? When I yelled at the prisoner second-in-command, he just looked awkwardly at the floor. Resolutely I walked up to our cell boss.

Even this rough fellow appeared to have been seized with something like emotion. "Don't get so excited, Stefan!" he said in an unusually quiet voice. "It was certainly better for him that way—"

Filled with anxiety, I clutched his arm. "What did you swine do to him? I want to know where he is!"

Roughly, but not nearly so brutally as usual, he pushed me back. "Quit bothering me about that old crackpot!" And with that he turned away. I then excitedly grabbed the man standing next to him, a younger Jew who hadn't been with us very long.

"Herr Keitelberg . . ." he hesitated, "took his own life. He cut his wrists; it must've happened last night, shortly after you were gone. Nobody heard or saw anything. When we got up this morning, he'd already bled to death. . . ."

THE DEATH OF the old man occupied me unceasingly for as long as I remained in Koronowo. Even with the much better working and living conditions, I could find no peace. I wanted out—I would have given anything in the world to be away from that dreadful place. . . .

Earlier, bare survival had taken up all of my attention. I could imagine only my next crust of bread, or a warm spot. In the writing room of Koronowo, my longing for a normal life reawakened—and my love for Willi, just as if it had all been the day before. The past year became like a bad dream. What had my letter brought about in Willi's life? Had he also been tortured—or even worse? Willi—if only I'd known if he were still alive. . . . I tried hard to believe he was.

At the beginning of 1944, before my escape plans could take more concrete shape, I was moved to the reformatory at Sztum—ostensibly because of good behavior. Later I learned that the Germans intended to "Germanize" some Poles. Since Mother was very much afraid that I might not be able to survive imprisonment, she'd entered a petition for my inclusion in the program, and thus I was among the so-called Population List Group III. This was the real reason for my transfer to Sztum, which enjoyed a considerably better reputation than Koronowo. Again and again I kept thinking, What would Mikolai say about this step?

When I arrived in Sztum, however, I experienced very few of its advantages. Suddenly I came down with an illness that I must have contracted in Koronowo as a result of the constant undernourishment and miserable conditions. A festering sore developed on my right leg, and it began to spread. The prison infirmary had no medications at all, because everything was being used for the armed forces.

Nevertheless the weeks in the infirmary at Sztum seemed like a luxury, for of course there we didn't have to work. There were twelve boys in all in my room. I was the only Pole. The others came from France, Belgium, and the Netherlands and were considered by the Nazis to be of "higher value." However, the other boys never made me feel conscious of this nonsense but were really okay. We were united by our rage against the Germans, who had not only occupied all our countries but had torn apart our families and thought they could train us to be "better humans" here.

On my left lay Jaap, a straw-blond boy, at most fifteen years old, from a small Dutch village on the North Sea coast. He had brilliant blue eyes and might have jumped straight out of a German propaganda poster. However, in his heart Jaap was far from dreaming of a German World Reich. Jaap's parents had both been active in the Resistance and had hidden a Jewish boy from Jaap's class at school in a room in their cellar. After a demonstration in Amsterdam, Jaap's parents were arrested, and he wounded a German soldier with a knife.

One night when the others were already asleep, Jaap hobbled over and climbed into bed with me and told me his story in whispers. I listened breathlessly to every word.

"And what happened to the Jewish boy from your class?" I whispered back softly.

"If only I knew that!" Jaap's brilliant eyes blazed even in the semidark. "When the soldiers banged on our front door, Pieter disappeared into his cellar hideout in a flash. After the fight with the one soldier, they just searched the house fast because they wanted to get their comrade to the doctor. So Pieter wasn't discovered. But he couldn't possibly have stayed in the sealed house after that. Man, I'd love to know where he is now too."

"And your mother?"

"I was kept separate from Mother in prison. Later I found out she was sentenced to ten years. A piece of luck . . ."

"What? That's luck?"

"I was so afraid they'd shoot her, too, like—" Jaap stopped, swallowed hard, and fell silent. I knew what he'd been going to say. Jaap would never see his father again.

From that night forward we were friends. Jaap said once that he didn't have the feeling for men that I did, but he could just fall asleep better if he was lying next to me. I'd never known anyone to be so marvelously uncomplicated as Jaap, especially not a boy who really was interested in girls.

Sometimes we giggled in bed like schoolgirls: Jaap was splinted almost up to the hip with a leg fracture, and since I also was bandaged from ankle to upper thigh, we really made a comical pair.

Unfortunately, sometime in the early summer of 1944, our nice time ended suddenly, though neither of us could know that we would see each other again months later. On that particular morning a guard, along with a doctor, came into our sickroom urgently looking for a few workers. He marched through the infirmary seeking out what he called malingerers.

Each of us tried anxiously to shrink down in his bed. When the fellow saw on the card at the end of my bed how long I'd already been here, he tore up the card in a rage and screamed at the doctor, "Man, don't you understand that this isn't any sanitorium? This rascal should have been back at work long ago!"

The doctor was no coward and replied firmly, "But the boy has severe inflammations, which under the present conditions simply haven't healed—"

The guard interrupted him in midsentence, tore off my covers, and bellowed at me, "Let's go—get up and come along!"

At my first attempt to stand on both feet, I immediately pitched forward full length. This appeared to irritate the guard even more: "If you're pretending, queer, you'll be disposed of immediately."

The doctor finally insisted that he must first change my

dressing. He would send me along later. I was just able to cast a last glance toward Jaap as I limped out of the room with the two men.

For the following weeks and months I was assigned to the work detail of that obnoxious senior guard, Petersen. I will never forget his name. He was from Hamburg and was a gay-hater of the worst kind. After a short time it was clear to me that he must have pulled me out of the infirmary on purpose, along with five other boys who'd also been sentenced under Paragraph 175.

Among his first actions was that at night, after work, he had each of us shut up in a solitary cell, so that we had no contact with the other prisoners. He had signs attached to the outside of our cell doors reading in huge block capitals: CAUTION—FORNICATION WITH ANIMALS!

Our work consisted of digging antitank trenches against the ever-advancing Soviet Army. Often the shovel was more of a crutch than a tool for me. Once, when I fell headfirst into the mud from exhaustion and had no more will or strength to pick myself up, he walked up close and hissed at me: "I know how creatures like you have to be treated—I learned from Höss in Sachsenhausen! I won't touch you. As far as I'm concerned, you can lie there and die. Only you'd better clearly understand one thing: If you don't run back on your own at recall, you'll be shot!"

To this day I don't know how I got back into my cell that night. Some fellow prisoner must have helped me. Any specific memory of it is gone.

There's only one outstanding experience in the months following that's worth mentioning. In September 1944 the news got through to us that units of the Polish underground army had risen against the now retreating German Wehrmacht—in Warsaw! This gave me courage. Though it didn't change anything about our daily lot, it gave us hope again, real hope that the war would end soon.

The Germans were able bloodily to put down the uprising in Warsaw. Almost 170,000 Polish civilians lost their lives in it, and some 70,000 more were dragged off to concentration camps or to slave labor. The city of Warsaw was largely leveled "in punishment." But the Red Army was already on the other side of the Vistula. Now the most important thing was to hold out.

FLIGHT ACROSS THE RIVER

B<small>Y THE END</small> of September 1944 we had finished digging all the trenches. Before the German soldiers were to take up their positions, our work detail was ordered into a barracks encampment in the vicinity of Grudziqsz, a city farther to the south. Petersen, that slave driver, was in top form as he drove us boys along the highway with his men.

The only comfort for me was that once, from a distance, I thought I'd caught sight of Jaap. At any rate, hobbling along in another group was a boy with straw-blond stubbly hair who looked damned like him. I didn't dare wave, for Petersen still kept a sharp eye on us "creatures."

Arriving in Grudziqsz, we found a joyous surprise: Senior Guard Petersen left us immediately after he'd delivered us. Whether he was properly relieved or simply took to his heels in the face of the advancing Soviets, I'm unable to say. We six "creatures" breathed more easily, at any rate—we'd survived the fellow!

At the transfer I was excused from the heavy work detail along with some other boys. My bandages and trousers were completely blood-soaked after the march, and besides, my extensive wound stank offensively. One of the guards who looked at my leg said, "Tch, boy, we haven't any luxuries like a medical station here anymore. But come with me—from now on you're working in Supplies. You won't be outside there, and the work is tolerable."

In comparison to the slavery at Sztum, the work in Supplies was almost a pleasure. "Supplies" meant custody of the last remaining clothes and tools in the camp. And still more important: Supplies was located right next to the kitchen. After just a few hours I'd found out that a bustling exchange business was in progress. For me it was helpful above all to again be able to get some clean rags now and then to bandage my wound.

After a few days I found out that Jaap really had come to Grudziqsz. Unfortunately fate had hit him harder this time: Despite his badly healed broken leg, he was ordered into the trench-digging detail. It wasn't until two months later that we found an opportunity to meet briefly behind the latrines. It was winter again by this time, and I was deeply alarmed when I saw how pallid and emaciated he was. His once-blond bristly hair was now almost gray. Only his marvelous blue eyes had not lost their brilliance.

"How good to see you again!" he greeted me heartily in his nice Dutch accent. We embraced like brothers. For once I was the older brother.

"Boy, you're just skin and bones! And are those all the clothes you have for this murderous cold?"

Jaap nodded indifferently. "Never mind, it'll all be over by next spring. . . . Hey, boy—then we're going to feed till we burst!"

That very night I managed to organize a few warmer clothes for Jaap out of Supplies. Although we arranged to meet regularly once a week from then on, he never appeared again at our secret meeting place. I began to be very worried about him. But it was simply impossible to find out what happened to him. I could only hope that he hadn't gotten sick. . . .

In the last days in Grudziqsz I had a big fight with the other boy who worked with me in Supplies. His name was Helmut, he came from Germany, and he'd already been there before I came. He was a strikingly beautiful boy, seventeen at most, who'd not only built up an elaborate black-market system but also offered his body from time to time to get food or other valuable things.

The night before, there'd been a quarrel between him and the cook, who visited him regularly. The cook had then reported him to one of the guards, and during an inspection several frauds were discovered. Although I'd been fascinated by his looks from the beginning, we still hadn't developed any real sympathy for each other. To this day I don't know whether he really liked men or whether his homosexual activities were only a means of survival for him, for which he was only too glad to avenge himself. Anyway, he told the guard that the irregularities had begun only since I'd been there.

We both got fifteen lashes. I was quivering with fury. When we were finally alone, I challenged him: "You rotten liar! Why'd you get me in trouble too? We've both let other people have clothes from Supplies, but you've done it much more and for much longer than I have. Why did you do that?"

I had Helmut by the collar and was ready to beat him up then and there. When I was just about to swing, I noticed how he was trembling and how the tears ran down his cheeks, although he didn't say a word. The sight of his face, pretty and yet so upset, stirred me so profoundly that I let him go and abruptly turned away to keep him from seeing it.

How very much I longed for Willi during this period. . . . Sometimes I thought that it all was so long ago that it had happened in another world entirely. Then again it would be so immediate, as if we'd just embraced in our shed, as if I could still feel his skin on mine. . . .

I tried hard to believe that we'd see each other again after the war. Of course my mind told me that he could as well have died on the Eastern Front as met death through my letter—but I simply was not able to believe either possibility. If only the war were over, if only I were free again, then I would soon find him.

In the middle of January 1945 we suddenly received orders to pack into crates all the things remaining in Supplies. Was the Red Army so close already?

On Saturday the nineteenth of January 1945, only a few days after my twentieth birthday, I sensed a desperate panic growing among the guards. Apparently the camp was to move the following week, and now an argument had broken out over whether they should wait or not. Finally the faction that wanted to leave the very next day prevailed.

In the general confusion a group of boys succeeded in escaping. However, three of the boys were caught in the vicinity of the camp and shot immediately. This was a clear warning to the rest of us.

When we assembled for the march, I had a surprise. For hours I'd been keeping an eye out for Jaap, but I hadn't seen him anywhere. Just as I was about to leave the empty warehouse with one of the guards, he suddenly appeared in front of me: Jaap! Even paler, even grayer, even thinner—but alive!

"Jaap, have I missed you! Where've you been keeping yourself recently, anyhow?"

"Shit," Jaap replied drily.

"I beg your pardon?"

"I almost shit myself to death! Diarrhea round the clock. Until there was nothing left. Then I had a high fever and was just about unconscious for two or three weeks. Well now—am I in time for the trip, or not?"

I was so glad to have him nearby again! We made up our minds not to let ourselves be separated again for anything until this damned war was finally over.

Our goal was supposed to be some sort of railroad line farther to the west, on which the whole bunch of us was supposed to travel "home to the Reich." How and where we would find it wasn't entirely clear, even to the guards. We wrapped ourselves up with every remaining rag of material as well as we could manage. Jaap and I wound each other's heads so that only a small slit for the eyes was left. Not really luxury, at thirteen below zero.

The first two days were the worst. First we followed the frozen Vistula in a northeasterly direction. There were very brief stops every few hours. Whoever fell asleep was done for. The guards repeatedly told us that anyone who fell behind or tried to escape would be shot. We discovered that first night that they weren't kidding. Two of us six boys whom Petersen had always referred to as "queer creatures" had become friends; they tried under cover of darkness to take a different road. We others heard two shots and never saw them again.

Most of the farms and houses that we passed had long been abandoned. Nevertheless two or three of our guards always went in with drawn pistols to search for leftover food. Once they did in fact find a gigantic basket of bread that someone must have left behind. Or perhaps the original owner was no longer alive. Anyhow, I still remember that we thought it was good of the guards to have shared this treasure pretty evenly with us prisoners.

Jaap and I could hold an amazingly good pace with the others, although we limped badly. But every one of us had a handicap of some sort, so our overall speed was not very impressive.

By the evening of the second day many of us had developed severe pains that affected us all over. Each step became torture. Some, including me, had feelings of dizziness; from a distance we must certainly have looked like a horde of drunks. Seven boys, among them two of our youngest, remained stuck in the icy snow that night. One of them even begged for a bullet because he couldn't stand the pain any longer. Even the hard-boiled guards couldn't bring themselves to shoot the helpless soul. This night would be the last for him and the others anyway.

At noon of the third day Jaap spoke to me for the last time on the march. "Stefan—we won't give up, will we?"

I only nodded my head grimly. My tongue had become so

swollen that even speaking had become an agony. But at least from that day on a kind of general stupefaction set in, so we really didn't perceive our surroundings or ourselves. Like robots we reeled through the icy winter landscape. The few bright hours of the day alternated with the long dark nights, without my being able to differentiate the individual days anymore.

My mind was concentrated on not losing sight of the back of the man in front of me, Jaap. Sometimes I saw pictures, colored pictures with garish colors that began to detach themselves from the dirty tones of the pattern of his jacket and dance wildly before my eyes. In my ears roared loud sounds that I couldn't silence even by shaking my head wildly. Yet I always had the most profound determination to put the left foot in front of the right, then the right in front of the left, then.

Later I found out that we marched this way for two weeks. To this day I haven't learned where we stumbled on the railway line. I only know that it was at night when the whistles and piercing squeals of braking train wheels cut through all the fantasizing. Strong hands shoved us like cattle into freight cars. A little later we were rumbling along the rails toward the west. I think I remember that my feet were still making walking movements for hours afterward. But that was surely a delusion; I can't explain it otherwise.

In the afternoon of the following day, the train stopped suddenly with a sharp jolt. The person beside me banged so hard against my injured leg that I awakened with the pain and reflexively pushed him back. When I opened my eyes, I recognized my half-frozen brother-friend, Jaap, beside me. Thank God, we hadn't lost each other!

At first I had no idea where we might have ended up. As far as I could see, we were in the freight yards of a large city in Germany. We were unloaded from the cars and loaded and unloaded twice more—from trucks to rattletrap cars, or were they small ferryboats? My eyes kept closing all the time, but I stayed awake enough to be sure that Jaap didn't get lost.

When I came to the next time, I was lying on a real camp cot under a scratchy blanket. To my shock I noted that I no longer had any clothes on, and that my leg was freshly bandaged with clean rags. Where was I?

Before I could look around properly, a gray stubblehead bent over me. "Well, have you finally had enough sleep, Big Bear?"

Jaap also had a blanket around his shoulders and was enthroned on a plank bed. Relieved, I gazed at him.

"We're on an island near Hamburg," Jaap continued. "Hahnöfersand—ever heard of it? An island in the Elbe for youthful offenders. Really very nice here, as far as I can judge. They do farming and stock breeding, you know?"

Pale sunlight entered the room through a dusty window. I realized that the window had no bars. Oh well, you probably couldn't get off the island without help.

Jaap further informed me that he'd already found work for us in the hog shed. "Isn't that weird? They actually still have pigs here!"

After a few days I was well enough to accompany Jaap to the pigpens. The animals weren't exactly fat. However, the administrators of the prison did make an effort until the last days of the war to maintain something like self-sufficiency on the island.

Ever more frequently now, even down on our island, we heard the big city of Hamburg being hit by Allied bombers. Often at night the horizon would be dark red with the fiery glare of the burning city. Once, Jaap said, "If only one of those things would explode over this mess!"

But I vigorously disagreed with him. "Listen—at the eleventh hour? Hey—it's just going to be days now! You'll see!"

Spring of 1945 came in with the first mild days. What a gift, after the horror of that terrible winter! But still there was no talk of an end to the war. The guards now often left our cell doors open during air raids. It seemed as though some of them had escape plans themselves.

At the end of April 1945, Jaap came running up to me late one afternoon when I was just finished with the daily mucking out of the pens.

"Stefan—toss the fork and come quickly. Two other boys were able to grab a boat that drifted ashore and asked me if I want to get away with them. I told them I'd only let one friend know fast and come right back. You'll come, won't you?"

What a question! The British as well as some Canadian units couldn't be very far. Repeatedly their planes had flown so low over us that we were able to read their national insignia and had waved madly toward the sky. Besides, we were worried that our guards might decide to put us out of the way at the very end, so we couldn't be unfriendly witnesses.

As quickly as we could, using the cover of bushes and trees, we ran out of the actual prison grounds, to an embankment on the shore of the Elbe. Good luck—the two boys had waited for Jaap and me. We jumped into the little old rowboat and paddled like mad with a pair of old boards in the direction of the shore. The current was so strong that we were carried a good ways downstream. But that didn't matter to us. Just to get away from the island.

At last the nose of the rowboat bumped against the river-bank. Overjoyed, we leaped onto the shore, ran up the embankment, and looked around to see if the enemy was anywhere nearby. When we could see no one far and wide over the flat countryside, we let out an exuberant howl. We were free! We had finally escaped our miserable imprisonment!

But where were we going to go from here? The two other boys were Belgians and, like Jaap, wanted to head west as soon as possible. And where should I go?

"You'll come to Holland with me, of course!" Jaap proposed firmly. "First we'll pick up my mother in Amsterdam, and then we'll all go back to our beautiful house on the North Sea together. You'll certainly love it there too!"

For Jaap it was a given that we would never separate again. But shouldn't I get home to Poland as fast as I could? If only Mother and Mikolai were still alive! They'd certainly be very concerned about me—it had now been many months since we'd heard anything of each other. And what had happened to Willi? Had he also been able to survive to the end of the war, as I had? When, when would we ever see each other again?

I couldn't go east anyway, since the last bastions of the German Army were still there, so I decided to go west, toward the Allies, with Jaap and the others.

We didn't know how far it was to the front lines from where we were, so we decided to keep going through the first night and then hide out somewhere and rest the next day. But as the day began to dawn, we saw a military camp in the distance. When we sneaked closer, we could see a slack British flag dangling from a pole.

Jaap, the only one of us who knew English, suggested that we should all just shout "Good morning!" loudly for as long as it took for the sentries to see us and recognize us as fugitives.

And that's how it happened. For the first time in years we all four got a proper breakfast—with fried eggs! Of course nothing stayed in our stomachs very long, but the taste had been simply heavenly. After that we slept all the way through till the following morning.

ONCE AGAIN I had to decide where to go. And again Jaap urged me to go home with him.

But in the meantime my plan had taken shape. I intended to write a letter to Mother and Mikolai that same day and give it to one of the officers with the request that he send it on to Poland as soon as it was possible to do so. I myself had decided to head south. I'd heard there were already regular Allied military transports from Munich to Vienna every two weeks. Vienna—would Willi already be there? I had to find this out for myself before I'd know where I might belong in the future. . . .

I AM STEFAN K.

Afterword to the
American Edition

THE LETTER TO Willi. I still feel under my hand the brown paper on which I set down my words in poor German. The letter that the Nazis used to imprison me and torture me. The letter that perhaps cost Willi his life.

I thought constantly of Willi after my flight from the prison island of Hahnöfersand, too. At first I was in the British occupation zone. Then I succeeded in getting to Munich with American soldiers, from whence I hoped to be able to go on to Vienna. In Munich I was admitted to a UN refugee camp and declared a Displaced Person, with the number G 0324 7480. Here I received the first humane treatment and medical help from Americans. To this day I remain grateful for it.

By that time I'd heard from Vienna that the Russians were still there and I would not be able to get there from Munich, at least for the time being. And furthermore, I'd realized that despite the liberation from Nazi rule, there would be no concomitant liberation for homosexual men and women for a long time. Perhaps I'd only cause new difficulties for Willi if he had in fact survived, if I were suddenly to turn up at his family's house in Vienna. But it wasn't only that. I was simply terrified of having to face the possibility that my letter had delivered him to the Nazis.

In the meantime I'd established written contact with my parents and brother and sisters in Toruń. My dear mother wished nothing more keenly than to see me once again before her death.

I've remained in Poland ever since. Until 1960 I had to; after that, although foreign travel did begin to become possible, I never went to Vienna. In the decades of Stalinism, I not only had to practice a constant double life as a homosexual, but also had to deal with some professional disadvantages. Still, I succeeded in gaining my high school diploma and graduating from a university. However, I could never practice my profession as an economist, the position to which my training really entitled me. Among other things, I was regarded as an "unreliable person," because I didn't return to Poland immediately after the end of the war and also because I continued to try to maintain contact with friends in the West, even with some American citizens. In 1980 I was retired at age fifty-five on a reduced pension for reasons of poor health, mainly a result of my Nazi imprisonment.

As a homosexual man, I've followed the recent growth of democracy in Eastern Europe with much hope and concern. One can breathe much more freely in Poland today, too, despite material problems.

Unfortunately my physical condition has been worsening considerably for quite some time. In the coming year I will be seventy years old.

With this background, I've been trying since the end of the eighties to obtain acknowledgment as a victim of Nazi persecution and to receive indemnification for time spent in Nazi prisons. So far all official applications to appropriate government agencies have remained unsuccessful, although my prison file card was found in the archives of the judicial authorities in Hamburg and it substantiated all my assertions to the exact day.

So much the greater, then, are the thanks due to German homosexuals, who sponsored a drive to collect money through newspaper appeals and public events. Among other things, this has made it possible for me to obtain Western medication, which I couldn't have afforded otherwise.

The letters from all the young readers of my story, which German-Dutch author Lutz van Dijk has faithfully recorded and which was first published in 1991 in German, have also been a special joy to me. Sometimes there are whole classes of schoolchildren who inquire anxiously about my health, and they often report that through this book they've learned something about the history of homosexuals for the first time ever. I'm very glad that young people are learning not only something about the persecution aspect but also about the aspects of love and friendship and the fact that it's important for every human being to stand up for his or her own feelings and desires. Some of the young people even want to help me with food packages or in similarly concrete ways. This has touched me deeply. A young doctor from Hamburg regularly provides me with medication. Once a German journalist interviewed me on the radio here in Warsaw. Through all this I feel that I have not been left alone.

STILL A WORD about my dear friend Willi: I've never forgotten him. However, it's just since the collaboration with Lutz van Dijk on this book that I began to search for him systematically. But all inquiries to archives in Poland, Germany, and Austria remain unsuccessful to date. My fear of a dreadful truth has not vanished.

To this day I have Willi to thank for my being able to experience feelings of love as something beautiful from the beginning. Beyond my own personal case, I believe that people in all the countries of this world must grasp that it is always a crime to punish love and to tolerate violence. The reverse is the only way that makes sense.

Stefan K.

Warsaw, November 1994

P.S. With the money that I received for this American edition, I will be able to fulfill my long-nurtured dream of another journey: I'm going to go to Israel. Besides Herr Keitelberg, who is referred to by name in my story, I'd previously had other Jewish friends who suffered with me. Most of the ones who survived the Holocaust went to the United States or to Israel after the war. I haven't forgotten any of them.

ACKNOWLEDGMENTS

First of all I owe my thanks to Stefan K., of Warsaw, for his courage and his trust, without which I could not have written this story.

For information I am grateful to: the Staatsarchiv, Hamburg; the Jugendanstalt Hahnöfersand, Hamburg; the Strafvollzugsamt, Hamburg; the Zentrale Nachweisstelle, Aachen; and the Bundes-Militärarchiv, Freiburg.
Furthermore, my special thanks for advice, criticism, and support are due to: Marcel Bullinga, Amsterdam; Professor Dr. Georg Hansen, Bremen; Rainer Hoffschildt, Hannover; Detlef Jahn, Berlin; Dr. Burkhard Jelloneck, Saarbrücken; Dr. Pieter Koenders, Amsterdam; Tamar Laakmann, Berlin; Jens Michelsen, Hamburg; and Professor Dr. Wolfgang Popp, Siegen.

Lutz van Dijk
Hamburg, April 1991

135

Notes on the Story

page 12. The Molotov–Ribbentrop Pact, a secret "non-aggression" agreement between Germany and the Soviet Union, was signed on August 23, 1939. As part of the deal, the governments agreed on the future division of Poland. The German assault on Poland began on September 1, 1939, followed by the "Western campaign" of the Soviets on May 10, 1940. On June 22, 1941, the German armed forces attacked the Soviet Union without a declaration of war, in violation of the pact.

page 16. During the period of the German Occupation, from 1939 to 1945, the Polish population was made to suffer heavy losses: Of a total of 35 million Poles, some 6 million lost their lives; of those around 3 million were Polish Jews. Of the 2 million Poles shipped to Germany as forced laborers, about half succumbed to the inhuman working conditions; many of those who survived sustained severe damage to their health. Neither the survivors of the dead nor those who still feel the consequences of their years of suffering have ever received any compensation, although many of the German firms that used Polish forced labor during that period are today earning millions.

page 30. During the Occupation, Poles were forbidden to be on the street after eight P.M. Passes were granted only to those who had to be at their workplaces later and could prove it.

page 53. With the widespread agreement of the Austrian people,

German military units crossed the border between the two countries on March 12, 1938. Two days later, amid jubilation in Vienna, Adolf Hitler announced the Anschluss ("union") of Austria and the German Reich. From then on Austria was called Ostmark (literally, East March). At the beginning of April 1938, the first concentration camp in Austria was established at Mauthausen.

page 60. The reference is to Dr. Magnus Hirschfeld (1868–1935), who had been active, even during the time of Kaiser Wilhelm, against the punishment of homosexuality. Dr. Hirschfeld also promoted a more liberal divorce law and the availability of birth control. In 1919, in Berlin, he founded the Institute for Sexual Science. On May 6, 1933, it was occupied by students and plundered, and its library was destroyed in the Nazi book burning of May 10, 1933. At the time Dr. Hirschfeld was in France, from whence he did not return. In 1934 he was deprived of his German citizenship. The doctor died in exile in France in 1935.

page 79. In Toruń / Thorn alone after 1939, as part of the political measures of the German Occupation, twenty-four Polish doctors were murdered. Aside from the scarcity of medications generally, there were very few medical supplies for Poles at that time (according to Czestaw Madajczyk, 1988: *Die Okkupationspolitik Nazideutschlands in Polen 1939–1945*, Berlin (East)/Cologne, p. 306).

page 83. The words of this letter correspond to the original, which the seventeen-year-old Pole Stefan K. sent to his friend Willi G., the Austrian-German soldier.

page 86. The concentration camp Stutthof, established in the region of Danzig in September 1939, had several outer camps, one of which was near Toruń / Thorn. Altogether some 100,000 people of various nationalities passed through this camp. Ten thousand died as a result of the hideous living conditions; thousands more were systematically shot in the neck in special areas designated for the purpose or, from June 1944, gassed.

page 94. On November 15, 1941, Hitler decreed that "for the maintenance of the purity of the SS and the police" their members, if found guilty of homosexuality, should be punished with death without regard to age (according to Hans-Georg Stümke, 1989: *Homosexuelle in Deutschland. Eine politische Geschichte*, Munich, p. 121).

page 103. Paragraph 175 was first included in the German penal code in 1871; it provided imprisonment for "sodomy that is committed between individuals of the male sex or of people with animals." In 1935, under the Nazis, the paragraph was sharpened and expanded with Paragraph 175a, which provided that even suspected "sodomy between men"—including the simplest manifestation of love, such as exchanged glances or love letters—was punishable, and furthermore that prison sentences of up to ten years could be imposed for "serious cases."

page 118. Höss refers to Rudolf Höss (1900–1947), who worked in the Sachsenhausen concentration camp as an SS officer and in 1940 was promoted to commandant of Auschwitz. In his memoirs, written in a Polish prison, he wrote about his "experiences" with homosexual prisoners in Sachsenhausen: "Neither very hard work nor strict supervision helped with these. . . . Many committed suicide. The 'friend' meant everything to these creatures in this situation. . . ." (cited by Martin Broszat, 1963: *Kommandant in Auschwitz: Autobiographishe Aufzeichnungen des Rudolf Höss*, Munich, p. 81).